DANCING THROUGH LIFE
BOOK THREE

A SLOW Waltz

PATRICIA M. ROBERTSON

Chapter 1

Ava was breathing harder and harder as the cool fall air burned through her lungs. She wanted it to burn away all her memories, free her mind of all the events of the past years. After the week she had had, all she wanted was some space far away from the demands of her world, especially her classroom. She could not tolerate one more pimple-faced pubescent boy, burping and farting in the back of her classroom, eliciting giggles and groans from those around him. She couldn't tolerate her life. It wasn't the life she had dreamed of back when she had been a pubescent girl herself.

With each step her head felt clearer as she left behind her problems. This was to be a new beginning, a fresh start in a new place. Why, then, did her problems cling to her like a bad haircut?

She loved running. While running, her life seemed manageable. She felt capable and competent, able to take on any challenge. So unlike her true self. She rounded the path, leaning into the curve and willing her body to go faster. Finding this bit of woods on the outskirts of town had been a godsend. She hadn't asked who it belonged to, didn't want to know, wanted to remain in blessed ignorance, assuming it was public property. Certainly God knew she needed this, a place where she could get away from prying eyes and all their questions. She needed this and God had provided so she wasn't going to question.

Her heart rate increased, pounding in her chest as she continued up the path, heading to the clearing she knew was ahead. She allowed her body to bend to the curves in the path, willing herself forward until she reached the top of the rise. It wasn't a mountain view, not like in her home state, but it still afforded a panoramic view of the town she now inhabited. She missed being able to see for miles at a time. In contrast, all of the rolling hills and forests of her new life felt claustrophobic, like they were closing in on her. Even the smells of the woods were different from the mountain air, surrounding her in a stuffy mist. But it also was a good place to hide.

She breathed in deeply, hands on knees as she bent over. A tree branch snapped behind her. She looked up and an ugly brown mutt in a bright orange vest ran up to her and attempted to lick her face.

"What?" Ava backed away, not trusting the bull dog face, crinkled as if in a grin, and the wagging tale that carried his body along with it. How dare he intrude upon her space?

"What are you doing?" The dog was followed by ... a pimple-faced boy, or at least that was what she had thought at first glance. A second look revealed that he was older than her eighth-grade students. A youthful face appeared under a hunting cap, his body enveloped in a large hunting jacket, a rifle cradled in his arm.

"Don't you know enough to stay out of the woods during hunting season?" He removed his hat and wiped his brow, revealing that he was even older than her second guess. "At least wear something bright orange to let hunters know you are not a deer. I could have shot you."

He looked her up and down in her black running pants and brown sweatshirt.

"Sorry, I thought this was public property."

"No, this is private property, my property. You are trespassing."

"I'm sorry. Where did I go wrong? I started at the park."

"You crossed into my property at the first rise. It's clearly marked."

"Well, I won't make that mistake again, thank you." Ava turned and began her run down the hill, her face crimson.

"Wait," the hunter called after her, holding his dog by the collar lest he follow after the departing figure. Too late. She continued down the path.

Dale shifted his rifle, squatting next to his dog, and rubbing Lucky's head as he watched after her. He hadn't meant to sound so rude. It wasn't like him. But then he didn't know what was like him any more. He didn't recognize himself, hadn't felt like himself since Joy had left.

It had been over a year since she had died. It still didn't seem real. She had been so much a part of his life. It was hard to remember a time when she hadn't been there. They had known each other since grade school. He got up each day, put one foot in front of the other, took care of the kids and went to work, but he was only half alive. Everywhere he looked were reminders of his wife, sights, sounds, even smells. So much had died with her. He believed in the resurrection. For every death there is a resurrection. Where was his, he wondered as he stood up and continued to watch the path that had held the young runner.

"Lucky," he whistled. The brown mutt had wondered off into the brush. He scampered back through the underbrush, covered with burrs.

"Some hunting dog you are. You scare away the deer with your chasing everything in your path, real or imaginary." Dale was just going through the motions of hunting. It was more about being out in nature than shooting a deer. The mustiness of fallen leaves invaded his nostrils, wiping away reminders of his former life. Here, in his woods, he was alone with his thoughts in a way he couldn't be in his home. There were too many traces of Joy in their house, the home they had built together. He thought about selling the house, but what about his kids? They had lost their mother: Must they also lose their home? So he had decided against it, at least for a while.

He wondered about the woman he had startled in the woods as he turned in the opposite direction toward home. He hoped she made it back out of the woods safely.

Ava made a quick retreat. Even this small escape was being taken from her, she thought as she ran, anger rising into her throat and then swallowed down. What right did she have to be angry? She was only getting what she deserved.

Chapter 2

Esther had mixed feelings about hosting Thanksgiving this year. She had often wanted to host the day in the past, but had conceded to her daughter-in-law. She hadn't wanted to get the day in the way she had. Last year Dale had held Thanksgiving in his home as he felt Joy would have wanted him to. This year he had relinquished the holiday.

"It was Joy's thing, you know, not mine," he told her. "You've always wanted the whole family over for Thanksgiving. Now's your chance."

Esther invited Joy's parents. At first Mary had thought she would be able to take back this holiday herself, but when her sons' wives insisted on going to their parents for the day, she relented and accepted the invitation. Joy's sister, Sara, and her husband were also coming. With Peter, her dad, her daughter Kathleen and the grandchildren, it would be a good-size group, a size appropriate for Thanksgiving.

"Can Uncle Howard come too?" Ashley had asked. Howard had become a part of the family two years ago with the introduction of his dog, Lucky, to the family. Now Lucky was theirs and so was Howard. Ashley had become especially attached to him this past year.

"Of course he can come. Let him know that. He's one of the family."

The aroma of turkey and stuffing permeated the house as her guests arrived, contributing to the festive occasion. Howard appeared, carrying his signature dish, green bean casserole. "Smells great," he said as he handed over his contribution to the feast.

As everyone was finishing the meal, trying to save room for dessert, Esther quieted the group down and kept the men from rushing back to their football game with her announcement.

"Wait, before all of you get up. I have some news, or rather, Peter and I have news." Esther paused, waiting to make sure she had everyone's attention.

"We're waiting, Mom. What's up?" Kathleen asked.

Esther reached into her pocket, pulled out a ring and placed it on her finger. "Peter and I are engaged."

"That's great news," and "Congratulations," came from all around.

"About time," Erick, Esther's dad added. "I'm not getting any younger. I would like to be able to walk you down the aisle."

"When's the wedding?" Mary asked.

"We haven't set a date yet, but we'll let you know as soon as we know."

"When are we having dessert?" Jacob broke into the congratulations.

Esther laughed, "As soon as we clear away these dirty dishes," she said as she jumped into action.

Later, as they were finishing the dishes, Esther asked, "Who's staying for the champagne toast?" This was a tradition Sara, Joy and she had started a few years back, after Joy's first successful round with chemo. It had expanded to include others over the years.

"Not me, Mom. I have to get the kids home." Dale bowed out.

"Me neither," Sara said.

"But why?" Esther asked.

"No drinks for me." Sara waited for her news to sink in.

"But it's a tradition," Esther began as Mary came over to her daughter and hugged her.

"I knew it. I knew there was something different about you."

Sara laughed.

"What are you talking about?" Tom asked as he came into the kitchen.

"Just that our daughter is pregnant, right dear?" Mary said as Sara shook her head yes.

"So much good news," Esther said. "All the more reason for a toast."

"We're going to Larry's parents tomorrow for a second Thanksgiving and to give them the news. We have to leave early so I hope you understand when we don't stay," Sara explained.

"Of course," Esther said as she said her goodbyes to Dale, her grandkids, and the rest.

"So, Kathleen, looks like it's just you, me and Peter." Esther turned to Kathleen.

"Sorry, Mom, not tonight. I've got plans."

"What do you mean you've got plans? What plans can you have on Thanksgiving that don't include family?" Esther started to say more then stopped as Peter put his hand on her arm. "Will you be late?"

"Don't know, Mom. Don't wait up." Kathleen made her exit. Josh and Scott, Kathleen's sons had plans as well. Her dad retreated to his room to sleep through another football game.

"I guess it's just you and me," Esther said to Peter. She opened a window to allow the cold breeze to sweep away the remains of the odors from the day's celebration before cuddling next to Peter.

"Is that so bad?" He squeezed her and poured them both a glass of champagne.

"Not at all, Peter," she said as they clinked glasses. "Not at all."

Chapter 3

Ava spent Thanksgiving alone. She could have gone home. She couldn't afford the flight but her parents would have paid to have their wayward daughter fly home. It was her choice to stay here, alone. That didn't make it easier. It would have been a hassle, flying all that way for such a short amount of time. Maybe over Christmas, maybe not. She wanted to be alone, wanted to punish herself. She relished feeling miserable. It felt good to wallow in self-pity. Tomorrow would be another day. Time enough to get off her butt and try to take positive steps and ... smile! How she hated all those people telling her to smile when it was the last thing she felt like doing.

"Fake it till you make it," Jenna, her college roommate had told her repeatedly. She was tired of faking it. When would she start to make it?

The microwaved turkey dinner fit her mood perfectly. It sat, congealing in front of her, until she dumped it into the trash. Instead she picked up a slice of pumpkin roll from the plate of cookies one of her students had given her.

She had had invitations for a "real" Thanksgiving dinner from the parents of her students who had taken pity on her. They couldn't pity her as much as she pitied herself. She was the pity queen. Maybe she'd finish off her meal of sweets with a bowl of ice cream. Or not. Maybe she would go for a run instead. Certainly she wouldn't have to worry about hunters on Thanksgiving Day.

She couldn't believe how stupid she had been the other day, running in those woods. Growing up in Nebraska she certainly knew something about hunting. Why did she think it would be any different here in the Midwest? They don't have the big game of her native state, but were every bit as serious about this avocation. Half of her class had been gone on the first day of hunting season, the hunters' holy-day, November 15. She knew it was foolish to go into any wooded area until the season was over. Why didn't it register in her brain? Maybe she had needed to run so much that she was willing to disregard the danger? Maybe she desired the danger?

She flipped on her TV but couldn't focus on the game, couldn't focus on anything. It was either go for a run, or spend the day on the couch finishing off that plate of sweets. She chose the couch.

Chapter 4

Kathleen was meeting an acquaintance, Naomi, and going out. She was having some luck with her business, helping seniors navigate the medical system. She even had eight clients. Not enough to pay her bills, but a start. At one point she had thought she would be able to set this up as a non-profit where she would be paid a salary by the organization and wouldn't have to charge the seniors she helped. When that didn't work out, she was able to find clients willing to pay for her services.

She met with them for an hour each week, went over bills with them and called doctor offices and insurance providers. She kept extensive records of each call, much as she had for Joy during her illness. She also ended up doing odd jobs, replacing light bulbs, reaching items from the top shelf, picking up groceries. She drew the line when asked to wash windows.

"You don't pay me enough to do that," was her response.

The hardest part of her job was getting out of her client's home after an hour. They would offer her tea or coffee and want to know more about her life than she was willing to share. The women wanted to set her up with their divorced sons or single nephews. She had managed to dodge these liaisons, however in the process she had met Naomi, another single parent, niece to one of her clients. Soon they were making the rounds at bars in a nearby city.

It was worth the drive to get away from her hometown to a place where, so far, no one knew her. Here she didn't have to worry about running into former friends and cohorts in crime from her high school days. Here she could enjoy some music and drinks away from the boring routine that was her life. There was no night life in Cascade Falls, unless you consider the Green Door, one of the local bars, a form of night life.

While she didn't miss her old life in Chicago, she did miss the excitement and the diversity of a big city. Naomi had her back, and she had Naomi's as they tried out different bars. Kathleen wasn't looking for a romantic entanglement, just a few laughs, a few drinks, then home again. She knew how to handle her liquor, carefully nursing her drinks so she could drive home safely, chugging along in her blue Ford Fiesta. She had earned enough over the past year to finally afford a car, her and the bank, freeing her grandfather's car for her sons to use. It wasn't much, but it got her where she was going and was economical.

Josh was off to college so now Scott shared the keys with his great-grandfather. Josh was home for the weekend, but that didn't mean he was "here." He had many friends to catch up with. Kathleen saw no reason for her to stay home after the obligatory family dinner. She heard that a jazz group she remembered from her time in Chicago was playing at a club they had not yet visited, so she made plans with Naomi for the evening.

Naomi squirmed as she looked about the neighborhood but Kathleen paid her no attention as she parked the car and they crossed the street. They walked into the darkened bar and realized theirs were the only pale faces in a sea of black. Naomi wanted to leave but Kathleen stopped her. She felt at home, like some of the bars she had frequented in Chicago. Cascade Falls was boringly white, at least the part she patronized. Not only did she miss the night life, she missed the ethnic diversity of Chicago. The music was just beginning, permeating the room with rhythm.

"Come on," she pulled Naomi after her. They found a table in a side corner where they could see the musicians but not be seen. Kathleen ordered a bourbon on the rocks and sat back to enjoy the music. She was surprised when tapped on the shoulder and turned to see the face of her assistant at the dance studio.

"Leticia," Kathleen said.

"Letty here," Leticia corrected her.

"What are you doing here?"

"I might better ask you that. You don't exactly fit in." Letty smiled in welcome, giving Kathleen a hug.

"Neither do you." Leticia had taken over the running of the dance studio after Joy's death. She had been a student throughout her youth, assisted Joy while in high school and had been hired part-time to help Joy when her strength was slipping away. She had been the most likely candidate for the position after Joy's death, when they had decided to keep the studio open. "You always struck me as classical music, not jazz."

"Who says I can't enjoy both," Letty's eyes shone. "My uncle runs this place. Sometimes I help him out. Others times I just come for the music. They have a particularly savage group tonight. I had to come hear them."

"Savage? Is that good?" Naomi questioned. Kathleen and Letty laughed.

"Come meet my friends." Letty led them to her table where they pulled up chairs. "These are my cousins, Leo and Douglas, and my friend, Tonya." Kathleen felt welcomed and at home with the young people and ended up staying till closing time, despite Naomi's protests. Before leaving she made plans with Letty to return the next night.

Chapter 5

Josh and Scott were headed to a friend's house for a party. With Josh home, Scott had to negotiate for use of their grandpop's car.

"Why can't I have the car? Don't you have friends with cars?"

"Because I'm older than you. I invoke the big brother right."

"It's not fair."

"Who said it was fair. It just is."

"Scott, let Josh have the car. He can drop you off at the party. Call him when you are ready to come home," Kathleen had intervened.

"Great, getting dropped off like a baby."

"And that you are, little brother," Josh said, putting Scott's head into his customary headlock. "Didn't you miss me?" he said as he rubbed his brother's head.

And as if being dropped off at the party wasn't humiliating enough, Josh decided to stick around for a while after running into some friends.

"It's bad enough I have to put up with him at home," Scott muttered to Stephanie who had gotten a ride with them. He had been enjoying having a room to himself and not hearing about Josh's athletic prowess at school. It seemed Josh had gotten all the talent God was handing out, leaving none for him.

Scott struggled to maintain a B- average whereas Josh had sailed through school achieving A's with minimum effort. Josh had been the athlete, playing football, basketball and baseball, whereas Scott didn't know his way out of the locker room. While Josh was gifted in academics, Scott was better with his hands, first following his grandpop around and now working after school for his uncle Dale in his plumbing business. He excelled in shop and was more interested in taking trade classes than preparing for a four-year college. His uncle didn't talk a lot, but he understood Scott without having to say a word.

"Not everyone is cut out for a traditional college. Not me, yet I've done well enough. You'll be fine," Dale had assured him. Scott was planning on getting his plumbing license and working for his uncle when he graduated.

"There are worst things you could do," was all Dale had said when Scott had mentioned it. He seemed pleased though. It was hard to tell with Dale.

Josh had all the friends and all the looks. Scott was shy but had a heart for the underdog, hanging out with special needs kids in school at lunch, helping them with bullies. That was how he had made friends with Stephanie. Stephanie had been a new girl, starting in October their freshman year after student cliques had already been established. He had thought she needed a friend. Now she was the popular one. He didn't know why she bothered with him.

"Uncle Dale," he asked his uncle one time after work. "Did you always know that Aunt Joy was the one for you?"

"Pretty much. Even when we were just friends in high school, I knew. I was just waiting for your Aunt Joy to realize it as well."

"Like me and Stephanie," Scott added.

"Who's Stephanie?"

"Just a friend."

"Right." Dale smiled.

There was also a wild side to Stephanie that he liked. Stephanie may have been the one with all the friends, but he was a stabilizing force in her life, helping to keep her grounded and out of trouble when she wanted to try something foolish, like drinking. Scot didn't see the appeal, but with Stephanie, he gave in one time and came to regret it after vomiting in the car on the way home and waking up sick. His mom had suspected. He could tell by the look she gave him that morning, but she didn't say anything. That had been last year. Josh had helped him out, covering up for him and helping Stephanie get home. He had cleaned up the vomit and aired out the car lest the odor give him away. He could be a good brother at times. Scott hadn't been drunk since then. The same wasn't true for Stephanie or Josh, but they handled their drinking so much better than he did. Yet another thing Josh was better at than him, drinking.

He sometimes wondered whether they were truly related. They did have the same mother. That he knew. But father ... That was questionable. The only father figures he had known were Grandpop and Uncle Dale. His mom had been absent for the first twelve years of his life. He had been raised by his grandmother and great-grandfather, or Grandpop, until a few years ago when his mother had appeared. He wished he knew who his father was. He used to fantasize about him. Maybe he was a famous baseball player or football star, or a millionaire. He tried to talk to Josh about it, but had been shut down.

"No one knows who our dads are, and maybe it's better that way."

"But don't you wonder sometimes? Don't you want to know?"

"No, better to not go looking for trouble. Probably some low-life Mom found." Scott jumped on his brother and tried to hit him, blows that Josh easily evaded.

"Don't say that about my dad."

"I could just as easily say it about my dad. We just don't know," Josh said, calming Scott down. "Sometimes, I used to pretend he was a war hero in the Middle East somewhere. I'd tell myself that was why he didn't come around. But then I realized it was better to just not think about it." Josh had been old enough to remember how his mom had been when they were kids. She hadn't brought any men around that he remembered, but had been gone a lot. However, that was then.

"Things are different now, better. Mom's different. Better to focus on that and forget about the other."

Still Scott wondered. He didn't know what to say when kids asked him about his dad. In grade school he had made up an elaborate story about how his dad was away working and would return some day.

"No, he's not," Jude, a neighbor kid, said. "You don't even know who your father is. I heard my mom say so," he had taunted. Scott had hit him, starting a fight on the playground. His grandmother had been called to take him home. It had been the only fight he had gotten into. Since then he had learned to avoid the subject at all costs. It didn't mean he didn't think about it.

When he tried to ask his grandma about his dad, her face puckered and she turned away from him and changed the subject, much as she had done when he had asked her about his mom. Eventually he stopped asking. But then one day his mom had showed up after a stint in jail. He wondered if his dad would show up someday.

Stephanie only had one parent, too. Her mom had died six years ago in a car accident. Her dad had not remarried, instead raising his daughters by himself while pastoring the local Lutheran church.

"I wonder why your dad hasn't remarried," Scott said once.

"Don't be ridiculous," Stephanie had responded. "Why would he?"

"Don't you think he's lonely?"

"Why hasn't your mom got married?" she asked back at him.

"Why would she do that?"

"Same reason my dad would." Scott had wondered at that. It hadn't occurred to him that his mom would ever marry. She seemed happy as she was. Was she lonely?

"If my mom married then I would have a stepdad. It might be nice to have a dad like everyone else," Scott said.

"Be careful what you wish for. Do you really want some stranger living in your home and telling you what to do? I know I don't. We are better off as we are," Stephanie insisted. Still Scott wondered. He wondered what it would be like to have a "normal" family like his other friends, like Uncle Dale and Aunt Joy, only now it was only Uncle Dale.

When he brought the subject up to Josh, his brother dismissed it. "Trust me, kid. We are better off as we are. We don't need another adult sticking their nose in our business. We've already got way too much adult interference. We've got Mom and Grandma, Grandpop and Uncle Dale. That's more than enough for me."

"And now we've got Peter," Scott added.

"Just what we don't need," Josh had grunted before turning over in bed and going to sleep.

"But what if Mom is lonely?" Scott said as Josh softly snored.

Scott remembered the conversation from time to time as he watched his mom go out at night. Maybe someday he would have a dad, he had thought. That had been last year. This year he was too focused on his own life to worry about his mom's, focused on trying to keep Stephanie out of trouble.

If there was beer at a party, Stephanie always sniffed it out. She had said she was going to the restroom, leaving Scott with some of their friends in the basement rec room. When she didn't return he went looking for her and found her upstairs on the back porch with kids from Josh's graduating class.

"What are you doing?" he asked as he smelt beer on her breath.

"Just having a good time," Stephanie said, reaching for another beer.

"She's all right. Why don't you go back to the losers in the basement, kid," one of the older boys interrupted.

Scott ignored him and tried to get Stephanie to leave with him. "Come on, Stephanie. This isn't our crowd."

"Who says so," a guy in a varsity jacket continued to interfere. "Let her stay."

"Is that what you want?" Scott asked.

"Scott, you are such a dork sometimes. I'm just having a few beers."

"Okay, one more beer – then we better go home."

"I'll make sure she gets home," varsity jacket said.

"Is something wrong?" Scott was relieved to hear Josh's voice.

"Nothing, dude. We were just telling the pretty lady we would make sure she got home okay, right guys?"

"I'll take care of getting her home all right. I brought both of them. I'll take them home. Come on Stephanie and Scott." Stephanie didn't want to leave, but went along as Josh grabbed her forcefully by the wrist.

"You don't know these guys like I do," he told them once they were out of the house. "They're trouble."

"I thought they were friends of yours," Scott said.

"No, not friends, but I remember them from school. They were losers then, and college hasn't changed them any. You should stay away from them."

"It was just a beer, Josh. You're as bad as your brother," Stephanie complained.

"Then you're lucky you have my brother around. You don't want to hang with them. I guarantee you, it wouldn't be just a beer."

"I'm not a child," Stephanie pouted.

"Then stop acting like a child," Josh said as he pulled up to her home. Stephanie jumped out without a good bye. Josh and Scott waited to make sure she got safely inside before heading home.

"She's a piece of work," Josh said, breaking the silence.

"What do you mean?"

"I mean, I'm not sure she's the best person for you to be hanging out with."

"She's okay. It was just one beer."

"Was it? Maybe this time, but next time it will be another, and another, or something stronger."

"It was just this time."

"Are you sure of that?" Josh knew better. "What about that time last year when you came home drunk?"

"Okay, so it was more than one time."

"I'm just saying, I think she's trouble. You want to avoid trouble."

"How do you know what I want?"

"I don't, but I know you. I don't think she's good for you. She's looking for trouble and she will find it one day. I don't want you to get hurt in the process. I'm not around anymore to get your back."

"I can take care of myself."

"I hope so, little brother," Josh said under his breath.

Esther was still up when they got home.

"You're home early."

"It was a lame party," Josh responded.

"Well, that's good. Remember we've got a lot of work to do tomorrow. Have to get the storm windows up before the snow flies."

"Sure, Grandma." Other families went shopping on the day after Thanksgiving, Black Friday. Their family got the house ready for winter, lugging storm windows out of storage in the basement. It was a tradition, not a favorite one.

"Mom home yet?" Josh asked before going upstairs.

"Not yet. She should be home soon." Josh wondered about that. Wasn't it enough he had to keep his brother out of trouble?

Chapter 6

Kathleen woke up refreshed after her evening out. It hadn't been late. Because of the holiday, the bar had closed at midnight. She was energized by the music and new people. She had a chance to chat with the lead musician in between sets, sharing stories about Chicago. They were playing again tonight and tomorrow. She didn't promise she would be back, but had still made plans with Letty to drive up together.

Even though it was a national shopping holiday, Kathleen wasn't participating. She had an appointment with Peter's mother, Nan, her first client.

"We missed you at dinner yesterday," Kathleen said as she came through the door.

"Just didn't feel up to it. Besides, Peter brought me leftovers. They will make a good meal today. He's such a good son."

Kathleen went through the eighty-four year old's mail, looking for bills, bank statements, notices from the insurance company. It was light this week, it being a short week because of Thanksgiving. She could have easily skipped the appointment, as she had with her other clients, except she enjoyed Nan's company.

"I suppose you know about your son's engagement," Kathleen commented. "What do you think?"

"I'm delighted."

"Oh."

"Aren't you?"

"Sure, of course. It's not like it's a big deal for me, just for my mom. Let's go over these bills from the eye doctor."

"Aren't you happy about my son being your stepfather?"

"Stepfather? That's an odd term. There's stories about wicked stepmothers, none about stepfathers. How would I know what to think? Besides, at my age, I don't need a stepfather."

"But if you did, Peter would be a good one."

"Sure." As good as any, Kathleen thought. "But I don't need one."

"Then how about a husband?"

"Whoa, what's got into you today? You are definitely feeling better," Kathleen joked and returned to business. A half an hour later she was on her way.

She hadn't given much thought to the possibility of Peter being her "stepfather." Wasn't there a statute of limitations in regards to "new" parents? Once you hit eighteen, or twenty-one, they don't count any more, right? Kathleen didn't know but it seemed right to her.

"So, if I wait till Scott is eighteen before getting involved with someone, it won't count as a step anything, right?" she asked herself.

That seemed like a workable time frame.

Kathleen decided to go to the dance studio rather than return home. It was more than a convenient excuse to avoid the ritual prepping of the house for winter. She had plenty of work to occupy her time. Always had more to do than could be done at one time. Going in over the holiday would give her a jump start on next week so that, just maybe, she wouldn't start the week already behind.

She pulled into the empty parking lot and proceeded up the stairs to her office. She stopped briefly on her way to look at the main classroom. She remembered her decision to keep the studio open about a year and a half ago, after Joy's death. It had seemed like Joy had been talking to her, encouraging her as she always had. Telling her, "You can do it!"

"Can do what?" she wanted to shout to the room. Joy's presence was no longer as strong as it had been at first, even in this place, this sacred space where Joy had spent so much of her time, where she had invested so much of her life.

If only she were still here. She would know what to do. But she wasn't, and Kathleen was left with no guidance. Her devotion to Joy had been enough to get her through that first year, but she needed more than that to continue. The building was still draining what little reserve of money and energy she had left. The last bit of the insurance settlement from her dad's death had been invested in keeping the building open – the money Esther had guarded so carefully over the years to pay for college for Kathleen's sons. It was bad enough that the building was sucking her dry, but it was also taking time and money from her sons and her mother. How much longer could she let this go on? How much longer could she keep this place open based on a memory, a memory of someone she loved? Sure, her mother was a willing accomplice in this doomed enterprise. Along with Kathleen, Esther helped run the building, managing the accounts, adding her own vision to the one Joy had left behind. Still, it had been up to Kathleen whether to keep the studio open. When would she call it quits and save them from further loss?

These thoughts were ever-present companions these days, except for her brief excursions out at night. It was only while listening to music, sharing a few drinks, that she was able to put them aside for a while.

How much longer could she, could they, go on? The building was bleeding money. It had been quite the showplace in its day, or so she had been told, not that she was interested. Howard delighted in regaling her with stories about the building. Built during the 1850's, it had been a department store for a hundred years, until downtown businesses started moving out to shopping malls. Then it had been converted into a restaurant, using the restaurant area from the department store as the basis for the kitchen. The owner had created a ballroom/banquet area on the second floor that took up the back half of the building, including the third floor. The front of the building included the loft on the third floor that had become Joy's Studio of Dance, and offices on the second floor. The building was a sturdy red brick with high ceilings and tall, arched windows.

"Best steaks in town," or so Howard had informed her. "My kids all had their proms in the ballroom, before it closed. I remember many a New Year's Eve, dancing with my Helen in the ballroom." Howard's eyes misted as they always did when he mentioned Helen. Kathleen had no patience for his reminiscences, but Ashley seemed to enjoy them.

"Why did it close?" she asked.

"Just couldn't make a profit. Cascade Falls is more of a blue-collar, middle-class town. People wanted cheap burger joints, not high-end restaurants. That was reserved for special occasions. And then the two main factories were closed down and the work shipped down south. Less people, less money."

The restaurant had been closed for over twenty years, despite a few attempts to revive it. The last owner had started to partition parts of the first-floor restaurant into possible retail space for small businesses and offices, but hadn't been able to complete the construction and necessary infrastructure.

So far she had been able to patch the holes and string together a business framework, but how much longer? They had to start seeing profit soon.

"But in order to make money, you have to spend money," Peter had assured her. He had offered to invest in the building, but Kathleen had refused.

"It's enough that mom has invested her life savings. I can't let another person be saddled with this monstrosity."

Peter had argued, and given in, only with the idea that he would fight again.

"You may have won this battle, but you haven't won the war," he quipped. Kathleen hated his war analogies.

He had been right though. She knew Joy's Center for Healing and the Arts would only be successful if she invested money into the building. But where to get this money? She couldn't approach Dale. He had already spent way too much of his money on keeping the building open while Joy had been alive. Now he didn't want to have anything more to do with it. He avoided the place and all mention of it, even though Ashley and Jacob still came over most days after school.

Dale would wait in the car for them to come out rather than go into the building those days he picked them up. He was only too happy to let others drop them off after he got home from work.

Most days he worked late.

"I have to make up for all the time I lost while Joy was sick," was his excuse at first, but it was a year later and he was still working late. Between Esther, Mary, Kathleen, Tom and Howard, there were always family members around to take care of the kids; when there wasn't, the pastor's daughter, Michelle, helped out. Somehow they had assembled a level of normalcy for the children. They were in their own home, going to the same school they had been going to, and were being watched over by loving adults. Certainly they were okay, Kathleen assured herself. Just as her boys had been okay during her absence. She needed to believe that.

The vision was to turn this old building in the heart of the city into a functional, profitable, center for the arts. Joy's Studio of Dance was just one part of that vision. One of the first improvements had been to add classroom space. Joy's focus had always been ballet. She only needed the one dance space to do this. Classes were scheduled with no overlap.

"If we are going to make it, we need more classroom space and more types of dance. Ballet is just not enough," Kathleen had said to Esther. "We can clear out these two smaller rooms upstairs, combine them to make another classroom. Then we can talk about adding classes."

Many of the improvements had been superficial, easy ones that only required grunt work. Kathleen enlisted the help of her two sons for these. They cleaned out all of the abandoned rooms on each floor and added a fresh coat of paint to make the room more appealing to possible renters. They had put out a sign in front of the building: Office Space for Lease – Joy's Center for Healing and the Arts; and looked for businesses interested in investing in the building. New businesses that bought in had the options of choosing their space and making changes to suit their needs. This way Kathleen figured she'd be able to afford the upgrades, especially the wiring and technology today's businesses required.

"But we don't want just any business," Esther reminded her. "We want ones that fit our vision."

"Yeah, yeah," Kathleen agreed, all the while knowing she would do whatever it would take to avoid bankruptcy.

So far they only had one tenant, a potter fashioning creations on his wheel. Far from enough to pay the bills, much less show a profit. Kathleen worried they would lose this tenant as well if they didn't get more traffic into the building. Sculpture and artwork were all fine, but they weren't exactly big money makers. They needed something more.

They leased the dance classrooms to a yoga instructor during the morning and the Breast Cancer Support Group Joy had started continued to meet at no charge in any room available. Leticia was working on setting up a small gift shop where they could sell leotards and dance shoes as well as cards, books and devotionals related to healing. It was all coming together slowly, but too slow for Kathleen. The only way they had managed to get by last year, besides draining Esther's accounts, had been by her not taking a salary and Esther only being paid for part-time work when Kathleen knew she was working more hours than was expected.

This couldn't go on. But what were they to do? They were only one major repair away from bankruptcy. As long as the sixty year old boiler kept churning out heat and the twenty-five year old roof remained water tight, they were okay.

Chapter 7

After spending Thanksgiving alone on the couch, Ava knew she had to get out and get moving. It just wasn't good for her, all this aloneness. Perhaps it had been a mistake, turning down those invitations. Then she would have been ready to be alone for the weekend when there were no invitations. Too late to do anything about it now.

It was hard, harder than she had expected, this move so far away from friends and family. It wasn't the first one she had made, but it was different this time. When she had gone to college, everyone else was pretty much in the same situation: away from home for the first time where they knew no one. So much easier to make friends in that situation. After graduation she had joined Teach for America. She had been sent to a school in rural Tennessee, along with two other teachers. Even though it was a new place, she had a built-in set of friends through Teach for America. They had shared an apartment and the struggles of those apprentice years of teaching.

That was where she had met Edward. Another teacher in the program, he had been a year ahead of her and more experienced. She had fallen fast and hard. He was a charmer. She had been twenty-six when they met. She had decided to stay for an additional year at the school in the Ozarks; he had transferred from one on an Indian reservation, looking for new conquests, new experiences. And conquer her, he did. She had been ready to be conquered. She had wanted to have children before she was thirty and so, easily fell into Edward's embrace.

They were married by the time she was twenty-eight, separated by the time she was thirty. The divorce had been final last year. She had known the marriage was a mistake the day after the wedding as he had blown up over some minor detail on the honeymoon. She had told herself she was mistaken, that she could make this work.

But Edward had roving eyes. At first she had felt delighted that his eyes had lit upon her, but once they were married, he had started looking again, ogling the bridesmaids at their wedding. The divorce was final last year but not before he had given her an STD – genital warts, which had led to uterine cancer and a partial hysterectomy. She still had her ovaries, but nowhere for those precious eggs to grow into babies. She would have left him sooner but had needed the health insurance she received as long as she was still considered his wife.

The doctor said she was cancer-free; they had caught it soon enough. But not soon enough that she would ever have children of her own.

She had stayed with her parents during the chemo and radiation but now she wanted to be far away from all she knew in order to grieve her loss and build a new life out of the ashes of the old one. Cascade Falls was as good a place as any to do this. Far away from her home in Nebraska, St. Luke's Lutheran school was as good a school as any to serve her purposes. It didn't pay as well as public schools, but those jobs were hard to come by. She wasn't all that religious, but her parents were. When home she attended church with them. The pastor knew part of her story, the most recent part about the divorce and cancer, and knew of her job search. So whenever he received notices about teaching positions in the Lutheran school system, he sent them on to her. With his recommendation and references from Teach for America, she was able to land this position.

While not mandatory that teachers attend the Lutheran church, it was preferred. Ava thought it better that she go every Sunday rather than raising any more eyebrows than she already had. The single women around her age viewed her with suspicion, seeing her as competition for the limited number of single men, especially the unattached pastor. When Ava showed no inclination towards dating, their suspicions eased somewhat, but they had yet to extend a welcoming hand. She had more luck with married women her age, but they were busy with families, small broods of preschool-aged children hanging on them, or chasing after grade school-aged kids. Another reminder of what she didn't have, would never have. The parents of her students were friendlier, though older than her. They smiled at her when they saw her in church and stopped to talk, much to their children's chagrin. Still she had yet to make a friend, had no one she could call to meet for lunch or dinner or a night out.

She decided to go to school and get some work done in her classroom, changing the bulletin boards in preparation for Christmas. She was surprised to hear footsteps down the hall, but figured it was the janitor.

"Hello." Ava jumped at the male voice, almost falling off the chair she had been standing on while reaching the uppermost section of bulletin board.

"Whoa, I'm sorry. I didn't mean to startle you," the man approached. "What are you doing here on such a lovely day?"

"I'm preparing my classroom for Christmas. What are you doing here?" Ava retorted, regretting that she had not locked her door.

"I saw a car in the parking lot and the outside door was unlocked so I thought I would check."

The voice was familiar, if the clothes not what she expected, jeans and a sweatshirt.

"Is that you, Pastor?"

"Last I checked."

"You look different out of your collar."

"That's good. I like to think I can discreetly go about my business now and then without everyone knowing me."

"I'm sure that rarely happens. Everyone knows everyone in this town."

"That's pretty much the case. And you're one of our new teachers." He stretched out his hand in welcome. "I'm sorry I haven't gotten around to meeting you just yet, beyond hello at church."

"That's okay." Ava didn't want to be noticed, especially by the pastor.

"No, it's not. I usually introduce myself to new staff before this. Would you like to come over to my house for lunch? Join me and my daughters," he quickly added lest she get the wrong idea.

Ava wanted to say no, yet she found herself agreeing to his invitation.

"It's the house next to the church. Come over around noon." He walked to the door then turned and added, "Oh, and I'm locking the outside door to the building."

Ava had wanted company, but not exactly in this form. She wished for a female friend, but a friend of any gender was better than none, she thought as she finished the bulletin boards.

After she was done, Ava walked over to the rectory, knocked on the door and was let in by the housekeeper who looked her up and down. Ava was all too aware of her appearance, ripped jeans and a torn sweatshirt that slipped off her shoulder from time to time. Not appropriate garb for visiting the church pastor.

"I'm Ava Schultz, a new teacher at St. Luke's. Pastor invited me for lunch." Ava tentatively reached out her hand, wondering if she would get past this guardian of the sanctity of the pastor's home.

"I'll see if the pastor is in," the housekeeper said, ignoring Ava's outstretched hand and leaving her to stand in the entry way with a wave of her hand.

"Ava, come in." Joe appeared at the top of the stairs then bounded down them two at a time with a smile. "Ava's joining us for lunch," he told Agnes who grunted and went back to the kitchen.

He led her past a dark dining room, into the sunny kitchen where Agnes was setting another plate on the table.

"If that's all, Pastor, I'll be on my way."

"Thanks, Agnes. I'll take care of the rest." He motioned for Ava to sit down while he called his daughters.

"It's so much brighter in here than in the dining room. I hope you don't mind."

"No, not at all."

Two teenage girls appeared at the door.

"Dad, I told you I wasn't hungry," the older of the two complained.

"At least come in here and meet our guest," Joe insisted.

"Whatever … then can I go shopping with Marla?"

"Who's driving?"

"She is."

"When will you be home?"

"I'll call you."

Joe thought for a moment. "How about I call you? I want you home for dinner."

"Whatever, Dad."

"Okay, and this is Ms. Schultz, the eighth-grade teacher at school." Stephanie did a quick nod then rushed out the door.

"That was Stephanie," Joe said, somewhat apologetically. "And this is Michelle." He reached for the other teenager slouching in the door way and brought her forward.

"I think I've seen you at the high school," Ava ventured. "Aren't you in ninth grade?"

Michelle nodded. Unlike her sister, Michelle was attending the Lutheran high school. Stephanie had rebelled in ninth grade and ended up at the public high school.

"And I think I've seen you after school with some of the younger children," Ava added.

"Yes," Joe intervened. "Michelle babysits for some of the younger kids after school. Isn't that right, Michelle?"

"Dad, can't I have a sandwich in my room?"

"But we have company."

"That's okay, Pastor," Ava said.

"No, it's not. It's rude."

"But Stephanie ..." Michelle started.

"It's okay," Ava insisted again, before Joe could put his foot down. The last thing she wanted was lunch with a surly teenager. She had enough of them in her classroom.

"All right, just this time," Joe agreed.

"No girl her age wants to have lunch with her dad and a teacher. I don't mind," Ava said after Michelle left. "It must be hard, raising two teenage daughters."

"We do okay."

"I'm sure you do," Ava agreed. "It's hard enough teaching them. Can't imagine raising them." Ava had chosen to teach eighth grade. That didn't make it easy. They were a strange, yet interesting group, having yet to form a unique sense of self. They would move as one, in a group, at school functions. They went to the bathroom together, clung to each other, especially the girls. The guys hung out together too, but not walking arm in arm the way the girls did.

"So tell me about yourself?" Joe placed sandwiches and bowls of soup on the table. "Mmmm, Agnes makes the best soup. I hope you don't mind turkey sandwiches, leftovers."

"Everything tastes wonderful." Ava drank down the soup, realizing how hungry she was, how much she missed home cooking.

"So," Joe waited for her to fill him in. Ava knew he was waiting. It was the inevitable question she always got. She knew it was pro forma. You'd think by now she would have an equally pro forma answer.

"Not much to tell. I graduated from the University of Nebraska with a teaching certificate. Go Cornhuskers." Ava raised her arms in a fake cheer. "I taught for four years in Tennessee with Teach for America, and now I'm here."

"This is a far cry from Nebraska and all that open space. How do you like it here?"

"Just fine," Ava started to say then felt guilty for lying to a pastor. "As well as I'd like any place just now. A little claustrophobic, all those trees and hills, but okay."

"Oh," Joe's eyebrow arched. Damn, Ava thought. Why did I have to say that? I'm not here for a counselling session.

Joe waited in case she wanted to say more. When she didn't, he asked, "Have you been able to make any friends, yet?"

Ava shrugged her shoulders.

"Maybe I could help, introduce you to other people your age. We do have a single's ministry at church."

"That's okay. I heard about them. I'm not looking for anyone."

"The singles ministry isn't for match making, if that's what you are thinking. It's just a chance for people under like circumstances to meet, talk, go out, make friends."

"That's okay, Pastor." It was bad enough her mom was always trying to match-make for her. She didn't want her pastor doing it too. Besides, he wasn't really "her" pastor yet. He was just the pastor of the church she was attending. It would take more for him to deserve the title pastor with her.

"So what about you?" Ava turned the table around on Joe. "Two teenage daughters, what else?"

"Not much."

"What about their mother?"

"She died in a car accident seven years ago."

"I'm sorry to hear that."

"Not as sorry as I am to say it. You'd think after seven years it would be easier." Ava was surprised by this admission. Certainly a pastor would know how to get over such a loss.

"I'm divorced, you know," she told him.

"No, I didn't, but I wondered why you weren't married."

"Well, it wasn't much of a marriage."

"We do have a support group for divorcees."

"Of course you do. Is there anything you don't have a group for?"

"If there is, don't tell me. I don't think I can handle forming one more group."

Ava laughed, relaxing and allowing herself to enjoy his company. It was nice to have someone to talk to, even if that someone was a minister.

Chapter 8

There's nothing quite like a beautiful fall day and tailgating before a Michigan State home game. Little did Sara know that when she married Larry, she was marrying into the quintessential MSU family. Larry's dad had season passes to the football and basketball games. March Madness was more than madness in his family. At least they didn't show up at games with green paint all over their chests. Just so no one suggests this to Larry, Sara thought. Sara was a fan, but not fanatical. Still she enjoyed the unhealthy foods, the drinking and the party atmosphere. It was especially fun when the Spartans won. They didn't always attend the games, giving up their seats for friends of the family at times, but they usually made it to the tailgate.

"It's tradition!" Larry insisted.

This particular tradition hadn't been setting too well with Sara since her pregnancy. Even before what she believed to be true was confirmed, she found her stomach roiling at the smell of greasy burgers and spicy brats. Beer didn't slide down as easily as it had in the past. A good thing. She had never been much of a drinker, but had joined in on game days just to fit in. Now that her suspicions had been confirmed, she no longer accepted a cold brew, opting for warm tea or cider instead.

As for the pregnancy, Larry's parents had been ecstatic at the news, as she knew they would be.

"Another Spartan," his dad had said.

"Well, we'll see," Sara had responded. Who knew where this baby would go to school, what he or she would be like? Plenty of time for that to unfold.

"Of course, my grandchild will be a Spartan. Have to keep up the family tradition. I'm starting a college fund next week," Larry's dad had insisted.

"Okay, Dad. But who knows? I mean, this baby might have a mind of its own," Larry had warned. "Let's get the baby born before sending him or her off to college."

Now that football season was over except for bowl games, Sara was grateful to have Saturdays to themselves once again. Much as she enjoyed the camaraderie of the games, it was nice to be able to sit home with her feet up, especially as her stomach expanded to fit the growing baby. Her due date was early June. She hadn't started to show yet, but she was already in maternity pants as her jeans were too snug. She had also felt a small shiver of life within her as the baby quickened. It was so small, Larry hadn't been able to feel it, but it was real none-the-less.

How she wished her big sister was around to share this experience with her. Larry was great, but he wasn't Joy. Joy knew what it was to grow a life inside her. Joy had always known what to say to comfort and calm her when she was troubled. Her mom was around, sure, but it wasn't the same. Mom had a way of saying the wrong thing. Sara realized she didn't mean it the way Sara heard it; still, it just wasn't the same. Joy had been a second mother to her – a cooler more up-to-date mother. Her own mother had been much older than her friends' mothers, having had Sara when she was in her forties. Joy had helped her bridge the wide gap between her and their mother. Now she was gone when Sara needed her most.

It had been terrifying at first, the thought of bringing a new life into the world. She hadn't given it much thought when she missed her period that first month. She had missed periods before, but when another month passed by without the monthly "visitor" as her mother had called it, she began to worry.

"What if?" she said to Larry.

"What?" Larry responded.

"What if I'm pregnant? That would ruin everything."

"What are you talking about? We want to have children."

"Yeah, but not so soon. We've hardly been married a year. We have no savings. We're still paying off student loans."

"You're worrying about something that may not even be happening. You don't know you're pregnant."

"No ..." Sara looked down at her stomach. There was no sign of growth. She had always been on the plump side. But something didn't feel quite normal.

"Let's not worry until we know for sure. We can find out easy enough. We just need to pick up a pregnancy test."

"Okay," Sara agreed. "I don't even have a doctor here yet." Larry hushed her with a kiss, wrapping her in his arms as he slept. Sara lay awake.

"Baby," she said the next day as she looked at the results of the pregnancy test.

"Baby!" Larry lifted her off her feet and kissed her.

"How can you be so happy when I'm so worried?"

"We'll be okay," Larry insisted.

"I wish I were so sure," Sara muttered to herself, shaking her head. If only Joy were here she thought.

The past year had been a mixture of emotions. There was the joy of being newly married, mixed with grief over her sister's death. It had been a roller coaster ride. One minute she was feeling happy, and then she would feel guilty about being happy. How could she be happy with her sister no longer in her life? How could she live through such a loss? Yet she did. She had Larry to hold her and support her throughout the year. It didn't make it all better, but it helped.

"I don't know how I would have handled this without you. I can't imagine how Dale is handling it," she had said to Larry. "I don't want to imagine it."

"Then don't," Larry had told her. "Try not to think about it."

That Sara did, sometimes successfully – others time, more often, unsuccessfully.

And now she had a baby to be responsible for. Another worry.

Chapter 9

Sara's mother, Mary, had gone home after the funeral and taken to her bed for a month. She stayed in the guest bedroom, avoiding contact with anyone, getting up only when she knew Tom, her husband, was gone or in the middle of the night when he was asleep. Tom would hear movement in the kitchen as Mary fixed herself something to eat, but refrained from venturing downstairs. He knew better, knew to give his wife the space she needed.

Meanwhile, he filled his days with taking care of Joy's children. It was a comfort to get out of the house he shared with his grieving wife and spend time in Joy's home. It brought her back to him. Dale, for his part, welcomed the help. Sometimes Dale found it painful, seeing Joy's face in his children's faces. It felt good to escape to work, knowing his children were being taken care of. He had known of widowers with young children who had felt the need to remarry in order for their children to have a mother in their life, but not him. His kids had plenty of mother figures around from his mom, his mother-in-law, his sister, Kathleen, and his sister-in-law, Sara, when she was in town.

No, he would never marry again, he told himself. There was no one like Joy. There would never be anyone like her. He had had one great love in his life; surely that was enough for any man. He didn't need to go searching after another. Still, at times his body ached. He longed to reach out and touch another warm body. He longed for the touch of lips, but he realized, it wasn't just any lips he longed for, but his wife's lips. There would never be another.

He remembered how Joy had insisted that he remarry someday. He had finally given into her persistence but had never meant it. What was a lie to someone who was dying? He had only agreed in order to ease her last days. Surely no one would hold him to that promise. In the face of death, you said many things. If it gave Joy some semblance of peace to think he would remarry, then let her have it.

After a month in bed, one morning Mary showed up at the breakfast table, just as Tom knew she would, dressed and ready to go out.

"Where are you going?" Tom asked.

"Where do you think I'm going? Someone's got to take care of our grandchildren." She went to Joy's and took her place in the rotation of child care providers, picking up baby Grace. Mary burrowed her head in Grace's hair, taking in the smell of baby powder and oil, cradling her in her arms as Grace squirmed. An active two year old, she wasn't about to stay still long for anyone, even grandma.

"Where have you been, Grandma?" Ashley asked.

"Never you mind. Grandma was just a little under the weather. Now I'm back," Mary replied.

"Are you better now?" Jacob asked.

Mary hugged him tight then said, "Yes, now that I'm with you."

With Mary back practically every day, Dale almost felt unnecessary at home. Certainly the kids were fine without him, he told himself. And so he was free to bury himself in his work, coming home many nights after dinner, putting the kids to bed, then staying up late watching old movies, ones he and Joy had loved. He dreaded going to bed and often fell asleep in the easy chair downstairs rather than making his way upstairs and sleeping in the bed he had shared with his wife.

This went on for weeks. On weekends he would go for walks with Lucky in the wooded area of his property, once again leaving his children in the capable hands of his mother or mother-in-law, or a baby-sitter. He still managed to make it to church each Sunday. At one point Mary had wanted to start taking the kids to her church, but Dale drew the line there.

"No, St. Luke's is our church. That's where the kids will go until they are old enough to decide for themselves." His mother helped him with the kids at church, either coming to his home first or meeting them there.

It had been difficult, going back to church after the funeral. At one point it seemed he had been bombarded with non-stop casseroles and lasagnas as well-meaning church members, and some not so well-meaning ones, brought over meals for him and his kids. He made a point of avoiding the single women, hoping to hook this new bachelor. He had counted on his mom to run interference for him.

Sometimes they were a source of humor, other times an annoyance depending on who ran into them.

"His wife isn't even cold in the grave," Kathleen had commented with a snarl. She had become very protective of her little brother. Howard, however, laughed at the parade of women, having had a similar parade of his own after his wife's death.

"Don't worry. They'll give up soon enough. Especially if you don't encourage them," he said. And Dale didn't encourage them. He wanted to be left in the cocoon of sorrow he had wrapped around himself. That made him even more attractive to some of the women, but eventually they got the message. Kathleen internally fumed as she watched this.

"Another reason I'm glad I don't attend church," she muttered. Kathleen had her own grieving to do. She had never had a friend like Joy. She had managed before without one, for many years, Kathleen told herself. She could do it again. But it was harder now. Before she didn't know what she was missing. Now she knew it all too well. She longed for another friend like Joy, but knew she wouldn't find it. Instead she focused on trying to preserve the dance studio that Joy had wanted her to have.

"How can I let Joy down?" Kathleen thought. "But how can I keep the studio open?" Joy hadn't known that Dale had been subsidizing the building so she could keep her dance studio. She had thought it was profitable. Would Joy have given the studio to her if she had known? Had she realized what an albatross it would be around her neck? Certainly Joy couldn't expect her to do the impossible?

Grace was too young to know much about what was going on around her. As long as she was fed and cared for, she was happy, easily going from grandma to grandma, accepting the care of others as her rightful due. If she noticed Joy's absence, it wasn't apparent. Perhaps this was because she was used to being taken care of by her grandmothers during her mother's illness. Ashley and Jacob appeared to be doing okay, especially that first year. They were more concerned about their dad, how he was faring, than themselves.

"Is Daddy okay?" Ashley had asked Kathleen from time to time.

"He's just sad. He's okay," Kathleen had reassured her.

"I'm sad, too. I miss Dad." Kathleen had been surprised at that. She had expected Ashley to say she missed her mom, not her dad.

"You mean you miss your mom," Kathleen had corrected.

"Her too," Ashley said.

When she tried to say something to Dale about it, he dismissed her.

"You must have heard it wrong. She must have said her mom," he insisted.

"I think I know what I heard," Kathleen asserted, but Dale continued in denial.

Jacob was more open about missing his mom. It took a while before he stopped asking when she was coming back. It was a relief because each time he had asked, had brought the wound back to the surface. And yet it had also hurt, Kathleen thought, when he stopped asking. Were they forgetting? Were the kids forgetting their mom and moving on with their life? That was another loss. Kathleen didn't want to move on.

On the anniversary of Joy's death, they had held a small ceremony and planted a tree in their back yard. Ashley had resisted participating.

"I don't want to plant a tree," she had whined. Dale insisted she attend. She hung back with tears in her eyes as they put the small seedling in the ground, just as they had put her mother's body in the ground. Ashley remembered that moment too well.

"Do you think mommy likes our tree?" Jacob asked.

"I'm sure she loves it," Dale said and hugged his son. Grace had played by his side, trying to get into the black soil that they packed around the tree.

Dale had wanted to mark the anniversary in some way. This seemed as good a way as any. Joy had loved trees, not as much as she loved to dance, but it was something she loved. Dale still resisted going to the dance studio. He had not attended the year end dance recital, even though asked repeatedly by Ashley. He had promised her, then found he couldn't go into the building. He had turned around and gone back to work.

"Where were you, Daddy? You missed it," Ashley had said.

"Sorry, Ashley. Something came up at work. I'll come next year. I promise," he lied.

Ashley knew he was lying, just couldn't put it into words. She had not been that interested in dance before this, but felt compelled to continue as if to make amends to her mom for all the trouble she had given her before. She was taking classes again this year but was torn. She felt she needed to do this for her mom, but felt her dad didn't approve. When Jacob had said he didn't want to take classes anymore, Dale had agreed. Jacob still came to the dance studio with Ashley after school, but he hung out with his grandma or Aunt Kathleen and didn't attend classes.

"There aren't any other boys in the classes," he had stated.

"Sure there are. Stephen and Joseph are taking lessons," Kathleen had said.

"They're babies."

"Let him be," Dale had insisted.

When the anniversary of Joy's death came and went, Dale thought maybe now it would stop hurting so much. Maybe now he wouldn't spend every waking moment of every day, thinking about her, missing her. He had been right, and that was even worse. When hours passed without him thinking about Joy, he panicked. When he couldn't remember every little detail of their life together, the way she crinkled her nose when she laughed or the sparks that showed in her eyes when she was angry, he felt like he was losing her again. He pulled out pictures to help him remember. He must never forget, he told himself. He wanted to hold on to his pain, for in letting go, he feared he was losing her.

He called Pastor Joe to talk to him about it. Joy had made Joe promise to do that which he would have done anyway, caring for Dale as one of his flock.

"You know what it's like to lose a wife. I want you to help Dale. He won't ask for help. You'll have to ask him, repeatedly," Joy had told him. Sure enough, Dale hadn't asked for any help. At least not at first. Joe made a point of talking to him each week after the service, repeatedly asking him how he was, asking if there was anything he could do. Eventually Dale took him at his word. After Joe had stopped asking, Dale asked to talk to him.

"How are you?" Joe began.

"It's been a year since Joy's death."

"I know. I remember. How are you doing?

"I thought I was doing okay, until one morning I woke up in a state of panic. I reached over and Joy wasn't there. It was as if I had forgotten."

"Forgotten she had died?"

"No, forgot her. I'm so afraid I'm forgetting her. I don't want to forget her, not ever. What do I do?"

Joe sat back in his seat for a moment. "You won't ever forget her. Can't possibly forget her. You know that, don't you?"

"On some level, I do."

"But you do have to let go sometimes. Let go of your memories in order for new memories to form."

"I don't want to let go of any of those memories. It kills me that I'm already forgetting so much. I don't want to lose a single memory."

"It's normal after the first year to feel you are losing your loved again as you start to forget, but you need to achieve a new normal."

"I don't want that."

"Yet maybe that is what you need." Joe paused to let Dale think about this before beginning again. "Sometimes you have to move on. It doesn't mean you ever forget. You just find a new way to relate. You find a way to live your life, while maintaining a connection with your old life in your memories."

"How do I do that? Is that how you managed after the death of your wife?"

Joe fidgeted at the mention of his wife.

"No, it's not the same for me. No two griefs are alike. With Janice I had to let go of the negative memories to achieve some sense of normalcy. Not make her bigger than she was. I also had to let go of my guilt around her life and her death. You have no reason to feel any guilt where Joy is concerned. You were a devoted husband to the end."

"Then why do I feel guilty?"

"You have to answer that one."

"Because ... Because I feel like there must have been something I could have done. Maybe if I had been stronger about her getting the treatment she needed. Maybe if ..." Dale couldn't bring himself to say out loud what he was thinking. He was thinking about Grace. Maybe if they hadn't had Grace, maybe Joy would still be here. What kind of father would think that about his own child, an innocent baby?

"Maybe what?" Joe asked.

"Maybe if we hadn't had Grace ..." Dale said. Joe was well aware of the circumstances around Grace's birth. Joy had been pregnant with Grace when the doctor had first discovered her breast cancer. One school of thought had been to abort the baby and treat the cancer aggressively. Joy had refused any discussion of this option.

"And if that had happened, you may have lost Joy anyway, and you wouldn't have Grace," Joe said.

"I know. I wouldn't have that beautiful baby girl, but maybe I would have had Joy."

"And maybe not."

"Maybe not."

"And even if you had talked Joy into this, which there was no way you would have, how would she have felt about it afterwards, and about you?"

"Oh, I don't know if she ever would have forgiven me."

"So you would have lost Joy either way."

"I guess so. Maybe so."

"There's no reason for feeling guilty as far as Joy is concerned. If you insist on feeling guilty, then go home and be the best father you can be to those three children of yours," Joe said.

Dale agreed but knew it would be easier said than done. Besides, they were perfectly okay with all the love they were getting from other family members. "Just as I was okay after Dad's death because of grandpa," he reassured himself.

Chapter 10

Leticia had been surprised to see Kathleen at her uncle's club. It was like a part of her other life was bleeding into this life. Leticia tried to keep the two separate. There was the life she lived with her parents, a life of respectability and order, a middle-class white life rather than a black life, she sometimes felt. She was okay with that. Her parents had worked hard to get out of the slums where they had grown up. Her dad was a lawyer, her mother ran the local United Way. Both had advanced degrees. Her mother had a bachelor's in social work and a master's in business administration, her father had his law degree. They were successful, middle class Americans, raising two successful, middle class American children.

Leticia's brother had gone on to law school, following in their father's footsteps. She didn't know what she wanted to do. She liked dancing, was enjoying running the dance studio with Kathleen, and had loved Joy like a sister. Joy had encouraged her in dancing when others hadn't. Her parents were okay with ballet as a side line to a successful career, but not as a career. Leticia had yet to decide what that career would be.

Then there was the other side of her, the one that loved hanging out with her cousins, going to her uncle's club. Her parents had not forgotten their roots; they just didn't want their children going back to them. They were cordial to family but made a point of making sure their children had all the advantages they could provide, including dance lessons, piano lessons, tutors in math, everything to put them on the fast track to success. They didn't want their children hanging out with people below their socio-economic level, even if they were family.

Still Leticia loved hanging out with her cousins. She lived a double life. There was the life she had with her parents which included many white friends, fitting into white society. And the life she shared with her cousins and other black friends. In one world she was Leticia, in the other she was Letty.

Leticia had been surprised by Kathleen's appearance at her uncle's club, Letty loved it. She was happy to ride with Kathleen the next night.

"My kids have other plans, so there's nothing to keep me from going," Kathleen told her as she picked her up at the parking lot of the dance studio.

"Do you think your parents would approve?" Kathleen asked.

"No sense in inviting trouble," Letty told her.

This time they stayed past midnight, enjoying the rhythm of the music and dancing till their feet hurt. Kathleen sat back and watched Letty dancing, the natural movements of her body across the floor.

"Have you thought about teaching that?"

"Teaching what?"

"Those moves you've got, girl. Maybe it can be another class." Letty laughed at the suggestion but Kathleen was serious. "What do you call it? It's not hip-hop? Is it modern dance? With an African flare?"

"More like Letty's dance. Those moves are all my own," Letty said and went back on the dance floor.

"Business good for you?" Kathleen asked Letty's uncle Delbert as he sat down at her table.

"Now it is. Wasn't at the beginning."

"I've heard it takes several years before a new business is profitable. That true?"

"Was for me. You've got to have a long-range plan."

"I don't have several years," Kathleen told him.

"Then come work for me. I can always use someone with a head for business to help me run my club."

"What about your son?"

"He's got a head alright, a big head, but not one for business. Has some idea about being a musician." He nodded at his son,

Jerome, who was sitting in on a few songs with the jazz band. "If you need a job, let me know." He handed her a business card.

"Thank you. Not right now, but maybe someday." Kathleen pocketed the card.

Kathleen eyed Jerome. He appeared to be around her age, had a mellow voice and an even more mellow saxophone.

"The ladies love a man with a sax," Delbert said, following Kathleen's eyes. After the set, Jerome and Clayton, the band leader, joined them at their table.

"Not bad for an amateur," Kathleen commented.

"And what qualifies you to judge?" Jerome responded.

"I'm just someone with a good ear for music. I know what I like. You're not bad."

"That's what I told him. If he spent a little more time on that sax, there just might be a place for him in the band," Clayton added.

"Now don't you be stealing my son away from me," Delbert said.

"Just saying. No one's talking about stealing. That would imply he was yours to begin with."

"You can't lose that which doesn't belong to you," Jerome added. "I'm my own man."

"Then start to act like a man and get a man's job," Delbert snapped.

"Whoa, now. I'm not about to get between a father and a son," Clayton intervened. "How about you buy an old friend a drink?" Clayton led Delbert away to the bar, leaving Jerome with Kathleen and Letty.

"So what do you do besides blow on that horn?" Kathleen asked.

"I help run the bar, not that my father gives me any credit for it."

"If you spent as much time running the bar as you do running your mouth, you'd own the bar by now," Letty said.

"Now don't you be running me down, girl, or I just might call your mama and let her know where her baby girl is spending her weekends."

"You won't be telling her anything she doesn't already know," Letty replied, but decided it might be time to leave. "Come on, Kathleen."

"Will I be seeing you again?" Jerome asked.

"Will you be playing that saxophone again?"

"I'll let Letty know when I do."

On the ride home she continued to talk to Letty about adding another dance class.

"You know as well as I do that we have to keep innovating, adding new classes if we are to survive. Look at Boyer's School of Dance. She has hundreds of students."

"That means more instructors, more overhead."

"Aren't you up to it?"

"Is that a challenge?"

"Call it what you want. Think about it."

"I will," Letty agreed when she was dropped off.

"We can expand our market, bring in more students." Kathleen was still talking as Letty slipped out the door.

"I'll think about it."

Ashley hadn't been sure about taking more ballet classes this year. She was bored with them, but felt she would be letting her mom down if she quit so she had signed up again. At nine years old, she was tired of waiting for the long sought after toes shoes and ready for something else.

Howard had gotten into the habit of stopping over at their house, ostensibly to see his former dog, Lucky, but mostly to hang out with Jacob and Ashley and eat Esther and Mary's home cooking. Sometimes he would stop by the studio and pick the kids up for Dale. He enjoyed the music and the commotion of the studio with young people bumping through the hallway, banging into each other, laughing, smiling.

"What's wrong?" he asked when he saw Ashley sitting off by herself after class.

"Nothing."

"I know that's not true. You can tell me."

"I'm tired of ballet. It's the same thing all the time. I'll never get point shoes."

"Not if you quit you won't. Is there something else you want to do?"

"No, that's the problem. If I don't do ballet, I don't know what I'll do. I like dancing, just not ballet."

"My Helen used to dance. That was how I met her. Have I told you the story?"

"Not that one." Howard was full of stories, many she had heard several times.

"She was just sixteen. I was stationed in Belfast after the Second World War. I remember seeing her dance on the green with her friends, Irish dancing. Have you seen that?"

"No, I haven't."

"It was Riverdance, before there was Riverdance. She was barefoot and the prettiest colleen I'd ever seen. A couple nights later, I was invited to dinner along with some buddies by a cook from a hotel we frequented. We had gotten to know him and he invited us to his home. Said he had been in the Navy at Flanders Field. He saw the waters turn red with the blood of American soldiers, fighting alongside them. He hadn't thought much of us Yanks before that, but since then he appreciated us and wanted to do something for us."

"I sat down to the meal and there, sitting across from me, was the colleen from the green." Howard smiled.

"I courted her and when I went back to the States, I sent her passage to join me as my wife." Howard stopped as he remembered the day he met his wife at the train station after her long boat ride to Ellis Island and catching the train from New York. How the sun had shown in her face as she stepped off the train and looked for him. It was a while before she saw him which gave him time to just look at her and see her face light up when she saw him. It was as if it were yesterday.

"And what has that to do with me?" Ashley asked.

"Maybe you could learn some Irish dancing. I bet you would have a knack for it with all of the other training you've had. It's popular right now."

"I don't know," Ashley replied.

"Just a thought. You don't know until you've tried," Howard said. "Ask your aunt."

"Aunt Kathleen," Ashley asked on the way home. It was Kathleen's turn to drive them.

"Mmmm," Kathleen mumbled, lost in her own thoughts.

"Do you think I could learn Irish dancing?"

"Irish dancing?"

"Yes, Uncle Howard told me about it. He said it's popular."

"I'll do Irish dancing," Jacob joined in from the back.

"What do you know about Irish dancing?" Ashley retorted.

"What do you know?" he mimicked back at her.

Kathleen let the idea rumble around in her head. It was popular. Would she be able to find an instructor?

"Maybe, Ashley, maybe. I'll see what I can find out."

Chapter 11

Once the pregnancy test had confirmed what she had feared, Sara set about getting to know as much as possible about the change that was happening to her. She sought out mothers at work and questioned them about local doctors and hospitals. The more she researched, the more she thought she might like to have a midwife deliver her baby. After the first appointment, the midwife scheduled an ultrasound.

"That will give us a better idea how far along the baby is and determine a more accurate birth date," the midwife had stated.

Sara was only in her fourth month but had blown up like a house in her mind. Was it any wonder she was irritable? She asked the midwife about this.

"Some women just show more than others."

"I don't remember my sister being this big this soon," Sara responded.

"The ultrasound will help us know why. Maybe you're farther along than we thought. You don't have multiple births in your family, do you?"

"No," Sara shook her head, "I've always been on the heavy side."

"You're carrying all the weight in your stomach though. You don't appear to be gaining too much. You weren't taking fertility drugs, were you?"

"No." Sara and Larry exchanged looks. They hadn't even been trying to get pregnant.

"Well, we'll know soon enough."

"You don't think," Sara asked Larry as they waited for the ultrasound.

"Naw, can't be. There are no multiple births in your family."

"No, but didn't your aunt have triplets?"

"Yes, but she had been taking fertility drugs and was in her thirties. It's probably just a big baby. A bouncing baby boy. Not only will he be a Spartan, he'll be a football player."

"Not funny, Larry. You try pushing a football player out of your orifice."

"Don't worry. Everything will be fine."

"But what if it is twins?"

"Twice the blessing."

Chapter 12

Dale was surprised to see the young woman he had seen in his woods before Thanksgiving at the Christmas pageant for his children's school. She was sitting with the eighth-grade class in between escorting different classes to the stage and giving directions. He had hoped to meet her again to apologize for being so rude. He approached her at the reception where she was serving punch.

"You're doing it all," he commented, sneaking up beside her, his hands in the pocket of his coat.

"What are you talking about?" Ava asked.

"Directing the play, corralling a bunch of eighth graders and now serving punch."

"Do I know you?" Ava looked at him.

"We met in the woods, remember? You were running. It was hunting season."

"Oh, yeah, I remember now. Didn't recognize you without your hunting jacket and dog." They stood awkwardly for a moment. "Would you like some punch?"

"Sure," Dale accepted. "I just wanted to apologize."

"For what? You were right. I was trespassing. I'm just glad you didn't shoot me," Ava smiled.

"Yes, but I didn't have to be so abrupt about it."

"That's no problem. I haven't given it another thought."

"Oh," Dale had assumed she had been as bothered as he was. "Okay then. I also wanted to let you know, you can run in my woods any time you want, outside of hunting season, that is. Even then as long as you wear bright orange."

"Thank you. I might take you up on that."

"You aren't from around here, are you?"

"No, I'm a cornhusker, Nebraska."

"Long ways from home. What brought you here?"

"This job, teaching at St. Luke's."

Pastor Joe joined them.

"I see you have met," he commented. Since that lunch he and Ava had been spending time together. It wasn't dating, they assured anyone who cared to ask, just spending time. It was mutually convenient. Both had agreed they weren't interested in dating right now. Having someone to hang out with relieved some of the pressure to date. If others believed they were involved they were less likely to try to fix either of them up. It was nice to have someone to do things with without the pressure of a "relationship." Or so Joe thought. He was pleased to no longer have to deal with dinner invitations which were just a poorly hidden excuse for matchmaking as he was introduced to an unmarried daughter or widowed or divorced friend.

Of course, with the new friendship came other complications as the church gossip network went into high gear about the young teacher the pastor was dating. If he chose not to dissuade them of this notion by telling the truth, who would blame him? He wouldn't give credence to such rumors by denying them. If anyone cared to ask, he would tell them, but oh, so much more delicious to spin lies and rumors than to seek the truth. He knew more than one person who liked to indulge themselves with the sweet taste of gossip. Let them have their fun. For now he enjoyed the reprieve from the constant attempt to find him someone.

They weren't spending that much time together. Just enough. He would stop and talk to her after school, accompany her to school functions now and then, and if this resulted in them getting a meal together, no one was the worse for it.

"Oh, yeah, well, it was nice meeting you again. Maybe I'll see you," Dale said, excusing himself. "I better round up my kids and go."

"Dale's one of my church members," Joe informed Ava. "He lost his wife over a year ago."

"Oh, I didn't know. Maybe I should have been more friendly," Ava replied.

"Don't worry about it," Joe said, but Ava decided to make a point of looking for him at church that Sunday. She didn't know how she could have missed him all those weeks. He was close to the front, three children in tow, one an active toddler. The other two she recognized from school. A woman sat with him, appeared to be his mother, she thought. Ava clung to the back of the church, not wanting to be noticed. She slipped out immediately after service was over, as was her custom.

"Why not stay for coffee hour? It's a good way to meet people," Joe asked her as she slipped past him.

"Not today," Ava replied and hurried home to her empty apartment. "Not today," she repeated to herself. Today she was going for a run. She wanted to be gone and back before Dale made it home from church to avoid any chance encounters. After seeing him at church with his children, she no longer wanted to talk to him.

Chapter 13

"I hate my life!" Stephanie stomped up the stairs and slammed the door to her room.

"You better get in that room and stay there!" Joe yelled up the stairs at her.

"Why, Dad, why?" Stephanie opened the door and yelled back down the stairs. "Because I'm ruining your image of your perfect family with perfect daughters?" Michelle came out of her room.

"There's your perfect daughter," Stephanie pointed at Michelle.

"What's going on?" Michelle asked.

"Never mind, Michelle, go back to bed." Joe started climbing the stairs. "And you, get back in your room," he directed Stephanie.

"With pleasure. I'm never coming out." Stephanie slammed the door again.

"It's all right, Michelle," Joe reassured his younger daughter. "This doesn't concern you. Go back to bed," he repeated as Michelle started to respond.

It had been a long night. It had started with a phone call from the police informing him that his daughter was in custody.

"But my daughter is here asleep," he turned over, looking at the clock and trying to wake up enough to understand what was happening. It was after midnight.

"Do you have a daughter named Stephanie?"

"Yes."

"And you are Joseph Michaels?"

"Yes."

"Then there's a young woman here who claims to be that daughter."

"Just a minute." Joe climbed out of bed and opened the door to Stephanie's room. No one there.

"I'll be right there."

It had also been a long night for Stephanie. She had snuck out of the house around nine-thirty, after telling her dad goodnight.

"I'm going to study in my room for a while."

She met Scott a short ways from her home. "My Dad's in his study. He never even noticed me slip out." Scott had been unsure about going to this party, but Stephanie had been determined to go.

"If you don't want to take me, I'll find someone else," she had told him. So Scott decided it was better that he went to keep her out of trouble.

"Where are you going?" His mom had asked him before he left. She looked up from the bookwork she had brought home with her from the dance studio.

"Just to a friend's."

"What friend?"

"Jeremy."

"Do I know him? Who else will be there?"

"No, you don't know him. Stephanie will be there and some other friends."

Kathleen had frowned at the mention of Stephanie's name, but didn't say anything. "Isn't it a little late to be going out on a school night?" She looked at her phone, nine o'clock.

"We won't be late."

"Be home by eleven." Kathleen trusted Scott. It was Stephanie she didn't trust.

Scott was concerned about Stephanie. Her drinking was getting progressively worse. And that was the times he saw her drinking. He wondered if she was doing more that he wasn't aware of. Somehow she had been keeping her grades up despite her partying. He was struggling to keep up his B- average.

He knew better than to say anything to his mom about it. She already didn't like Stephanie. He had tried talking to his Uncle Dale about her, stopping by his office after work.

"Is there something wrong?" Dale finally looked up from his paperwork after Scott had waited for ten minutes without saying anything.

"What if someone had a friend who had a friend, who he knew was drinking?"

"Do I know this friend?"

"Oh, it's not me, but if someone I knew did, what should that someone do?"

"That depends. Is that friend in danger of being hurt or hurting others? How often does this friend drink and how much?"

"I don't know, a couple times a week, maybe."

"That's an awful lot for someone who's not supposed to be drinking in the first place."

"Should I say something to her dad?"

"If it was my daughter I would want to know."

"Yeah, but then this friend might never talk to me ... er, my other friend that is, again."

"Hard choice to make. But if this someone got hurt or hurt someone else while drinking, how would your friend feel about that?"

"Terrible."

"I think your friend has some hard choices to make." Dale looked over at Scott, "Can I help in anyway, help your friend that is."

"No, thanks, Uncle Dale. I'll tell him what you said."

The party was at the home of a senior, someone Scott didn't know.

"How did you get to know about this?" Scott asked.

"Friends of friends," Stephanie told him. "Come on, don't be a loser." Scott didn't feel good about this but didn't want Stephanie going alone. Once inside, Stephanie ditched him, slipping off to join other friends.

"Where are your parents?" Scott asked Jeremy.

"Out of town for the week. Lucky for us, huh?" He offered Scott a beer.

"No, thanks. I'm driving."

"Suit yourself." Jeremy went back to his friends. Scott wandered around the party looking for Stephanie. He found her in the family room, sitting on a couch, surrounded by people he didn't know. She was regaling them with stories.

"Stephanie, it's time to go," Scott shouted over the noise.

"What do you mean? The party's just starting," a burly senior intervened.

"I said, it's time to go," Scott repeated, ignoring the comment.

Stephanie finally looked up at him. "Scott, you are such a dork. Can't you see I'm having fun?"

"I see that." He pulled her off the couch and away from the group. "Can't you see that this group is just trouble?"

"You're not my father. You aren't even my boyfriend. You can't tell me what to do."

"I am your ride."

"I can get another ride home." Stephanie turned to the group around the couch. "Right, someone will give me a ride?"

"Sure, Steph," a voice responded.

"See. You don't have to stay on my account." Scott wished Josh were here. He wondered what Josh would do, but suspected that Josh would tell him to leave without Stephanie.

"She's trouble," he could hear Josh saying. But Josh wasn't here, and Josh wasn't his father.

"I brought you here, I'll make sure you get home safe," Scott said.

"Suit yourself, but I'm not ready to leave yet."

Eleven came and went. Scott had left the party to hang out in his car. After one more unsuccessful try to get Stephanie to leave, he was ready to give up when the police showed up, breaking up the party and rounding up any who had been drinking.

"You been drinking, Scott?" Officer Nash was a friend of Peter's.

"No," Scott told him.

"You're not lying to me, are you?" He smelled Scott's breath.

"No, I'm not, sir."

"Okay, you can go."

"But what about Stephanie? I have to take her home."

Officer Nash looked over at Stephanie who was stumbling and resisting arrest.

"That young lady is not going home with anyone. She's going to jail. We'll be calling her parents."

Scott was finally persuaded to leave.

"It's past eleven." His mom had been waiting up for him.

"Sorry, Mom."

"You haven't been drinking, have you?" Kathleen eyed him suspiciously and smelled.

"No, Mom."

"Well, you missed curfew. Are you okay?" She had been preparing to scold, then thought better about it.

"I'm fine, Mom, just tired."

"Okay, well get to bed. This time I'll let it slide, but don't make it a habit."

"Thanks, Mom." Scott was relieved to be home safely but felt terrible about leaving Stephanie. The next day the whole junior and senior classes were talking about the party and the arrests. Scott was surprised to see Stephanie.

"I didn't expect to see you today."

"No thanks to you. My dad's grounded me for life. Part of my punishment was coming to school with a hangover."

"That's not my fault. I tried to get you to leave."

"Look, just leave me alone. I'm tired of you trying to 'protect' me. I don't need protecting." Stephanie brushed him off and joined her friends from the party where they shared notes on jail and their parents' punishments. Being arrested boosted Stephanie's reputation among certain students.

"Scott, do you know anything about this party last night? A number of students were arrested for underage drinking," Esther had asked him that night at dinner. Kathleen looked at Scott but didn't say anything.

"No, Grandma."

"I hear Pastor Joe's daughter, Stephanie, was one of them. You're friends, aren't you?"

"Not really," Scott said. Again Kathleen looked but didn't say a word.

Chapter 14

Kathleen looked at the disparate group, gathered to talk about the future of the dance studio. Already she was thinking this was a bad idea. Already she was feeling her control being taken away from her. As much as she complained about the burden this building was, it was still her burden. She wasn't willing to let just anyone take that away from her.

They were adding new classes in the New Year, had already added several pre-ballet classes for pre-school students, using the new classroom space. There was a demand for this, more as an additional form of child care than an actual dance class. The classes consisted of moving to music and clapping their hands. Leticia had recruited teachers from the older students, thereby keeping the cost down. The hope was that these additional classes would eventually feed more students into the other classes. But even so, it wouldn't be enough, Kathleen knew. If they didn't add different dance classes, they would lose students as they became bored with ballet, just as Ashley had grown bored. She wasn't the first student to complain.

Kathleen had talked Leticia into getting further training in jazz and modern dance to eventually teach these classes. In the meantime Leticia had been able to secure teachers. Kathleen had managed to find someone willing to offer Irish dance lessons at the studio. It had not been easy and it was expensive. The instructor was coming from over an hour away. He demanded a certain number of students and to be paid per student to make it worth the drive. Kathleen had assured him of this and had searched for students. She wasn't going to make much money out of the class, but they were the only dance studio in town offering these lessons. She was hoping to capitalize on the popularity of Irish dancing not just to fill the class, but to bring more people into the dance studio where maybe they would take additional classes.

At one point she thought she might have to sign Josh and Scott up for the classes to get the required number, but as word got out through the schools and churches, she had her full class. Ashley had been the first to sign up. Even Jacob expressed interest. Kathleen had made the circuit of local churches and the schools, asking permission to post flyers on bulletin boards.

"We don't post flyers about non-school, non-church related activities," she heard repeatedly, but occasionally she heard extra words, "but I guess in this case it won't hurt, just this once." There was even interest among a number of high school students.

"If you are going to add classes, why not ballroom dancing for adults?" Esther had asked as she and Kathleen and Leticia had discussed the prospect. "Peter and I have been looking for ball room dance classes to get ready for our wedding. I'm sure there are other couples who would like to do this as well. And we could offer them on Friday night so they won't interfere with the other classes. It could be a great date night."

"You find the instructor and we'll do it," Kathleen had told her. Esther contacted some instructors and set up two sections of dance lessons for eight weeks each, one running from mid-January through mid-March, the second during April and May. "After that we can decide about offering more," she said.

This was a start but it wasn't enough.

Kathleen and Leticia had met with Leticia's mother, Alicia, because of her background in business and non-profit organizations. Leticia was the one who had proposed setting up the center as a non-profit. Kathleen was skeptical.

"Just because its non-profit, doesn't mean you can't make money or have to work for little to no wages. It's still a business and businesses have to make ends meet," Leticia had told Kathleen to assuage some of her concerns.

"But wouldn't I have to give up ownership of the building?"

"Yes, the non-profit would own the building, but you could be the executive director and still run everything. And maintaining and keeping up the building wouldn't fall solely on your shoulders."

"How so?"

"You would have a board of directors responsible for helping you with fundraising and overseeing all aspects of the business. But if turning over ownership of the building is a problem for you, you could set up the non-profit as separate from the building. They could pay rent to use the building," Alicia added her explanation to Leticia's

"That sounds more like it," Kathleen said.

"But then you would still be responsible for maintenance and repairs," Alicia said.

"Sounds like I would be regardless of how we do this," Kathleen responded. "Tell me more. I certainly know about making no profits," Kathleen had joked. She had no experience with non-profits. She had some training and background in business from her associate degree and her experience so far running her business, but none as far as non-profits were concerned.

"It's really not that much different from a for-profit business," Alicia explained. "As I said before, they are all still businesses and need to operate like a business, paying bills, salaries, having a balanced budget. A non-profit is not owned by an individual but by a board. You don't have to pay taxes, and donor contributions are tax-deductible, which is helpful for fundraising. There are also grants you can apply for and other funding opportunities."

"Being able to fundraise would be a plus. Do you know how hard it is to get people to spend money on any form of the arts when the economy is bad?" Kathleen said.

"Girl, I run United Way. You don't have to tell me about the bad economy," Alicia stated.

"But there are grants available specifically for the arts," Leticia interjected.

"Yes, but that's not exactly easy money. First you have to find the funders, then you have to write a compelling grant application and sometimes, no matter how well written or how worthy the cause, you don't get funding. It's highly competitive. And then there are strings attached, especially with federal money."

"Ma, are you here to help us or talk us out of this? Because if it's the latter, you are succeeding."

"I'm not trying to talk you out of anything. I just want you to know what you are getting yourself into," Alicia said. "So tell me, what is it you hope to do?"

Kathleen looked at Leticia. This was her idea. All Kathleen wanted was to keep out of bankruptcy.

"Wouldn't it be great to have a place where anyone can study the arts, not just people with money? And not just dance classes, music, performance, art. Wouldn't there be grant money available for this? Everyone benefits from the arts, but those who are poor . . ."

"Economically challenged," Alicia corrected her daughter.

"Okay, economically challenged, rarely get the benefits because their parents can barely put food on their table, much less afford music or dance lessons and all that includes – instruments, shoes, dance outfits. Wouldn't it be great to have a center like that where children who wouldn't ordinarily get to attend those classes could have lessons for free?"

"You don't have to sell it to me, baby. I think it would be wonderful if you can make it happen. But can a community our size support such a project? Or more important, will they with all of the competing demands for funds?"

"That's what we were hoping you could tell us," Kathleen said.

"I'm not saying I don't like the idea. There have been other ideas, just as good, that have failed."

"Why?" Kathleen asked.

"Hard to say. Timing, poor planning, or they just didn't have the resources they need. What kind of community support do you have?"

Kathleen looked at Leticia. "None, I guess. There're the current students, their parents."

"That's not enough," Alicia said. "If you are serious about this, the first thing you need to do is get together a group of community members and see if there is sufficient support to make this happen."

And that was how this group came to be gathered at the dance studio.

The group included Kathleen, Esther and Leticia as staff. Esther had invited Peter and Pastor Joe.

"Why do we need them?" Kathleen had questioned.

"Peter's invested in this not just through me, but from his years as a probation officer, and Pastor Joe's on a number of boards. Besides, he's my pastor. I want him involved." Kathleen had agreed. Leticia had invited the senior pastor at her church and her brother, George, the lawyer, for legal advice. Pastor Joe brought a young woman with him. Kathleen didn't know her but took an instant disliking towards her.

"This is Ava Schultz, a new teacher at St. Luke's," Joe introduced her. "She has a minor in the performing arts. I told her about your project and she was interested."

"I thought you might want to incorporate theater into it," Ava explained. After too many months alone, Ava was ready to start getting out into the community.

There were also a number of parents of students, some of the older students, and three members of the Breast Cancer Support group.

"We want to ensure Joy's legacy continues," they said. They had come in response to the notice Kathleen had posted in the building. She hadn't expected such a response. Maybe there was more support than she had thought?

And there was Howard.

"I need something to keep me busy in retirement," he said. He had spent Christmas in Florida with his sister, but this year had decided to return north for at least part of the winter. "There are too many widows down there looking to get their claws in me," he had said when he returned. "I'm better off up here with all you youngsters," he told Esther and Mary. "Besides, I'm needed here." Howard had started to fill his time doing small maintenance jobs around the center. Every little bit helped.

"Where do we start?" Kathleen asked, unsure what to do now that she had the people gathered.

"You tell us. You called the meeting," one of the parents said.

"Is the dance studio going to close?" another asked.

"No, not at all. That's what this meeting is for. We need to figure out what to do to not just keep the studio open this year, but to secure its future," Esther said.

"Maybe if we start by everyone introducing themselves and saying why they are here," Joe intervened. Facilitating groups was his area.

One after another, those in attendance talked about how important the dance studio was to them and their children. More importantly, they talked about Joy and all she had meant to them. It was as if she were present in the room. Kathleen held back the tears that were forming behind her eyes, stubbornly refusing to acknowledge them. Others weren't as stubborn as tissues were passed around.

"What do we need to do?" all asked after they had been introduced and had their chance to talk.

"We could fundraise," one parent offered. "Sell candy and baked goods."

"That's a thought, but it wouldn't be enough," Esther said.

"Aren't the extra classes enough?" another parent asked.

"They help, but not enough. We've got this whole building to maintain and not enough renters," Esther said.

"One possibility would be to create a non-profit organization to operate out of this building. But to do so, we need a committed group of people, people willing to serve on the board of directors, people willing to help with fundraising, grant-writing," Kathleen added.

"What would be the mission of the non-profit?"

Leticia stood up to address this, "To ensure that all children, regardless of their economic background, have a chance to experience and learn the arts."

Before the evening was through, they had the beginnings of a board, a fund-raising committee and a shared vision.

Chapter 15

Kathleen may have not known much about non-profits but she was going to remedy that. She signed up for a class on non-profit management at a local college, and another on business management to supplement the courses she had already taken.

"Why don't you go for your bachelor's?" Peter asked when she told him about her plans.

"I'm thinking about it," she told him.

She tried to talk Esther into taking the classes with her but Esther refused.

"I've got enough education to handle the bookkeeping. That's enough for me. Besides I've got a wedding to plan." Then Kathleen asked Leticia to take the class on non-profit management with her. Leticia had been taking courses in social work, following in her mother's footsteps, but remained uncertain about this path, so she had taken the year off from course work.

"A course on non-profit management would be a great compliment to a social work degree," Kathleen prodded her, enlisting the aid of Leticia's mother to get her back in school. Alicia had been none too happy about Leticia taking a year off.

"You've come so far, baby. You can't drop out now," Alicia had insisted when Leticia had given her the news last spring. "What are you going to do? You aren't going to hang out with that no-good brother of mine in that bar, are you?"

"No, I'll be working at the dance studio."

"Like that will pay the bills," Alicia had mumbled.

"It will pay all the bills I have right now and give me some time to figure out what I want to do. You wouldn't want me to graduate with a degree and then decide it's not what I want to do with my life."

"A solid liberal arts education never hurt anyone," Alicia argued.

"Let her be," Leticia's dad had intervened. "Not everyone is like you, knowing just what they want to do with their life."

"I didn't know exactly what I wanted to do with my life at her age. I just knew I wanted out of that ghetto. Education was my ticket out."

"Well, Letty is already out. She doesn't have to have that ticket."

"Without that ticket she could end up back where we started."

"You don't really believe that, do you?"

"If she hangs out with Delbert and his cronies."

Cliff decided not to honor that statement with a response. "You do what you need to do, honey," he told Leticia. "I have confidence in you."

Leticia wished she had the same confidence in herself. She loved how her dad always called her Letty. It was a term of endearment coming from his lips. She loved how her dad supported her in her endeavors, even when he didn't always understand.

There had been a time when she had thought about a career in dance. Her mother had been dead set against it. Her father, while unsure, had at least been willing to let her try.

"What would it hurt?" he said.

"And have her dreams crushed? How many African-American ballet dancers are there in the American Ballet Company?"

"There's that one ... can't remember her name. Didn't they do a 60 Minutes segment on her? She had had a single mom, lived in the projects, was a protégé of some sort?"

"She's the exception."

"The exception that makes the rule. Perhaps our daughter can be an exception too?"

"She's no protégé."

"Then she will find out soon enough. She doesn't need us to clip her wings before she even starts."

Joy had believed in her. She had encouraged her to try out for Juilliard. When Leticia didn't make it, Joy had pushed her to try again, but by then Leticia had other interests.

"Do you want to try out for Ballet Magnificat?" Joy had asked. "I still have connections there."

Leticia had considered it but decided it wasn't for her. Much as she loved ballet, much as she loved Joy, she couldn't see herself doing it for the rest of her life. Ballet was a good discipline, but it was so restricting. She loved the beat of the street, hip-hop, rap, jazz, but she couldn't tell her mom that. Maybe her dad would understand, but even he would draw the line there.

Strangely enough, Kathleen was the one who seemed to understand. Leticia wasn't able to put her finger on it, but it had something to do with incorporating the rhythm of the street with the discipline of ballet. She had heard about a dance program at a university in Detroit where they were doing this, crossing all disciplines of dance. They offered weekend dance workshops. That was what she wanted to try but she knew the money would not be forthcoming for any such lessons from her parents. Too impractical, her mother would say. And while her dad would not be as openly negative, he, too, would balk at spending so much hard-earned money on something that would reap no benefits that he could see. If she was going to do this, she would have to find the means to pay her own way.

In the meantime, the dance studio might be an avenue for her to provide opportunities to other young women. Just as Joy had believed in her, she believed in her students.

When she had mentioned the dance workshop to Kathleen, she had said. "Go for it! It sounds great."

"But how will I pay for it? My parents won't approve. It would also mean me taking weekends off. We don't have anyone to teach the advance ballet classes on Saturday morning."

"You don't worry about that. I'll take care of getting someone else for those classes. And I'll see if I can find the money to pay for your lessons. This is precisely what I've been talking about. You learn all that free style or whatever it is that's so popular, and you come back and teach it here."

Leticia had been excited at the prospect. The workshops were one weekend a month.

"You can stay with Sara," Kathleen added. "She would love having the company. She has way more room in that old house to ramble around in than she can use. It will be her contribution to the studio."

"Okay," Leticia agreed with a conspiratorial smile. Her parents need never know.

Chapter 16

Now how was she going to afford this, Kathleen thought the minute it was decided.

"You have to spend money to make money," she kept telling herself. She didn't have the money to pay her own salary. How was she going to pay for dance workshops?

As it was, Kathleen didn't have the money to pay for her business classes.

"Have the studio pay for them," Peter had suggested.

"With what money? The money I haven't got to pay my salary?"

"As a board member, I have a problem with our Executive Director not being paid a living wage."

"I'd take minimum wage at this point. I made better money working at McDonald's."

"It's only for a time. Keep track of your hours. Once the center is profitable we'll pay you back wages."

"Like that will happen."

"Sure it will. I happen to have connections with the board chair."

"You are the board chair."

"See."

Kathleen laughed despite herself.

"I would love to be paid, but by the time I pay the staff and all the bills, there's just no money left."

"You should be the first person to be paid. I will take it up with the executive committee. At least let me help you with tuition."

"No, I already told you, no. It's enough that you are co-signing this loan for me." With Kathleen's time in prison and lack of credit, she was not able to get a loan on her own. She had no collateral for a loan so that left her with only one option, a co-signer. Esther had offered to take out a second mortgage on her home to help with bills at the center, but Kathleen had refused. Esther didn't know where Kathleen was getting the money to keep the place open, even though she handled the bookkeeping. She knew Kathleen had been refusing to be paid.

"Until we start seeing a profit, then I don't deserve to be paid. Besides, this is my mission, Mom. You know, like all of the volunteer work you do at the church," Kathleen had assured her mom. "I'm making enough with my business," she lied.

"I don't see how you can with only eight clients, and none of them rolling in money."

"I'm exploiting them, Mom. Look at all of the homemade cookies and pies I've been bringing home. And I don't have to declare them on my taxes."

"Then maybe you can start paying room and board," Esther commented.

"I didn't say business was that good. I'll start paying you as soon as you pay me for all the work I do around the house, and the work Josh and Scott do. The way I see it, you've got three unpaid slave laborers for the cost of a roof over our heads and food."

The reality was that Kathleen wasn't making it. The money she made from her clients barely covered her auto payments and gas. Her trips out were funded by sharing expenses with first, Naomi, and now with Letty, and free drinks. She would buy her first drink and nurse it. After that she usually never had to pay for another. Kathleen didn't like the situation but it was what it was. She knew that the only way she was managing was by living with her mother. It wasn't a great space to be in, almost forty and still living at home, but she didn't expect it to last forever.

By taking classes she had qualified for student loans. She would have had to go full time to get grant money. She didn't see how she would be able to do that, not with her clients and working at the center. The loan paid for tuition, books and some living expenses. Kathleen readily accepted that, figuring there would be money enough to pay it off once the center was profitable. And if not, she could always disappear the way she had years ago. Kathleen kept that option in her back pocket. She wouldn't do it as long as Scott was in high school, but once he was on his own, in college, what would there be to keep her here? Not Joy, not any more. Not Dale, he hardly talked to her since Joy's death. Maybe her mom, but she had Peter and would be okay.

The loan co-signed by Peter was to cover needed repairs to the boiler.

"I patched it up best I could, ma'am," the mechanic had told her. "I don't know how much longer I can keep her going." He had given her a break, donated his labor, in exchange for dance lessons for his daughter.

"Thank you, Brian. You're a miracle worker."

"Hardly. There are some things even this miracle worker can't do." That had been December, over Christmas break, before having a board of directors. She had delayed paying the bill as long as possible, but now it was due. Kathleen had managed to keep the expense from her mom by keeping a separate set of books. As far as Esther knew, they were struggling but they were getting by. Kathleen wasn't sure about having a board of directors checking her books, but if there was anything Kathleen was good at, it was numbers, running numbers and cooking books. She kept a careful account book hidden in her office with all of the expenses that were accumulating. She added the cost for Leticia's dance classes to the account. If Esther knew about this, she would insist on a cut in her pay, as well as that mortgage. Kathleen would have none of that. Esther didn't need to know.

She told Peter the loan was for school. He didn't know about the student loan she had taken out as well. Before the money was due, the center would be profitable, she would get her back pay, and no one need know the truth.

So many ideas were floating around in her head. It was hard to keep track of all of them. While her newly formed board of directors was finding its way, focusing on mission, Articles of Incorporation and applying for 501c3 status, she couldn't wait around. She was still looking for renters to keep the doors open. She struggled to know what to do first, where to place her energy.

As Kathleen sorted through all that needed to be done, she remembered that moment in the meeting when everyone had been sharing how Joy had touched their lives. She remembered how close Joy had felt at the moment. She hadn't wanted to feel that. It was too painful. She would not allow any tears. She remembered another moment, a year and a half ago, when she knew Joy was gone. How she had seen Joy in her mind being picked up and carried off by a man who looked like the Jesus of her childhood. She had asked him, "What about me?" She had tried to put it out of her mind, didn't want to think about it. It was too painful. Still the question came back to her, "what about me?"

Why did Jesus take her friend? Why had he left her, abandoned her? Far better that she go than Joy. Joy had done so much good during her time on this earth, whereas she had been nothing but trouble. She had been terrible to her parents, especially her mom after her dad died, when her mom had needed her the most. But she had just been a kid. What did she know about death and loss and adult pain? What did Ashley and Jacob know? No, she didn't deserve to live, yet here she was. It would take more than a lifetime to atone for all she had done.

What about her? What was she to do? If she blew this chance, there would be nothing left for her, no reason to keep trying. She might as well return to the life she had led before coming home.

"What about me?" she kept asking, even as she refused to allow herself to grieve.

Chapter 17

Dale found himself hoping to run into the young woman in running clothes as he sauntered through the woods each weekend. The solitude he had so craved no longer satisfied. It was starting to feel oppressive. He had run into Ava the last weekend during his morning walk. Lucky had alerted him to her presence as he ran barking ahead of him.

"Hey there," Ava said as she stopped to pet the playful dog.

"Hey there," Dale echoed as he approached. "I see you've taken me up on my offer."

"Didn't have a better one," Ava said with a smile, squatting next to Lucky as he tried to lick her face.

"Oh, I don't know about that. Aren't you seeing the pastor?"

"Rumors. We're just friends."

"I'm glad to hear that," Dale said.

"Are you?" Ava smiled as Dale realized what he had just said. Was he actually talking to a single woman, even flirting? It felt like cheating.

"Yes, or no. The pastor is a great guy. He deserves someone in his life. Why not you?"

"So I've been told repeatedly, but believe me, it isn't me." Ava continued to pet Lucky as they talked. "I saw you at church. You have a beautiful family."

"You go to St. Luke's? How come I haven't seen you?"

"I try to stay in the back, out of sight. But I saw you. You have three kids."

"Right, Ashley, Jacob and Grace."

"Pastor Joe told me about your wife. So sorry for you."

"Yeah, well, I am too, but what can I do?"

"How did she die?"

"Breast cancer. It developed while she was pregnant with Grace."

"Oh," Ava said. Joe hadn't told her this. Somehow she had missed that part of the story. She clutched her chest and gasped for breath.

"Are you all right?" Dale asked.

"I'm fine, just fine. I better be going," she stopped petting Lucky and stood up.

"Oh, okay. Maybe I'll run into you again sometime, or maybe at church. Are you sure you are all right?"

"Sure, maybe," Ava said as she turned and began her run away from him.

"Here, Lucky," Dale called the dog. Lucky appeared ready to follow after the departing figure. "Come on, boy," he said again, grabbing Lucky by the collar lest he take off. They both watched her disappear into the woods.

Chapter 18

"Where do you want to go to eat?" Peter asked.

"Is this another one of those games where you ask me where I want to go, but you really want me to guess where you want to go?" Esther responded.

"No, where do you want to go?"

"How about Red Lobster?"

"Oh." Esther could hear the disappointment in his voice.

"What's wrong?"

"Red Lobster doesn't have keno."

"So what you really meant to ask me is where do I want to go that has keno?"

"No, that's fine."

"We aren't going to the Green Door," Esther said, naming Peter's favorite local dive.

"How about that new sports bar that opened downtown?"

"Fine, we can try it," Esther agreed.

"Now that's my girl," Peter said with a smile as he turned the corner.

Esther was happier than she had been in a long time. Some days she felt guilty about it. How could she be happy when her son was miserable?

"A mother is usually as happy as her unhappiest child," her own mother had told her years ago. She hadn't believed it then and now knew it wasn't true. Was she somehow less of a mother for being so happy? It had been so long since she had had a man in her life, and Peter was ... Peter was Peter. He was everything she had wanted in a man. He was great. Compassionate, caring, intelligent, and had a sense of humor. It was so nice to have someone to share her heartaches with.

"A grief shared is a grief lessened," her mother had also said. This time she had been correct. It helped to have a strong shoulder to lean on, a kind voice speaking words of comfort. And Peter was good with her kids, not that it was such a big deal at their age. Still it was nice to know they not only were okay with this relationship, but they got along with him.

"Will Peter be moving in here?" Scott had asked over dinner a few weeks after the announcement.

"Don't know. We would have to sell his house. What would you think of me giving you the house?" she asked Kathleen.

"I hadn't thought about it," Kathleen said. Peter had a small three bedroom, ranch style home. Room enough for Grandpa, but not her and the boys. It hadn't occurred to her that she might be homeless after her mom remarried. All the more reason to get her finances in control.

"Nothing's been decided yet. We are still talking." It would be a lot to ask Peter to move in here, Kathleen thought. He wasn't just marrying her mother, he would be inheriting four generations of family in one house. That was a lot to ask of anyone, even someone like Peter.

"I like coming over here," Peter had told Esther whenever she apologized for the commotion that was part of her family. "I like being around young people who aren't in trouble," he smiled over at Scott. Scott squirmed. Did Peter know something he wasn't telling?

His own children had moved to other cities. He didn't get to see them as much as he liked. It was nice to have this extended family. And Kathleen was good with his mother.

Peter was aware of what he was marrying into, and even happy about it. He smiled more readily and there was a lightness in his step that even the other probation officers noted.

"What kind of Kool-Aid is he drinking?" one had asked.

"He's in lo-o-o-ve," another said, drawing out the word in a drawl, as they laughed. Peter ignored them as he smiled to himself. He hadn't been looking when he first met Esther. She had just been the mother of one his parolees. He wasn't sure exactly when he had noticed her. Maybe it was after rescuing Kathleen from herself that first time when they had found her at her father's grave. There had been something about Esther. Maybe it was the damsel in distress look she had given him that time, but he had never been one for weak women. He didn't like women with a victim mentality. He had enough of that with his parolees, women intent on blaming everyone and everything but themselves for their situation, women who tried to manipulate with tears.

Kathleen had none of that in her, and neither did her mother. He appreciated Esther's strength and yet that glimpse of vulnerability where her kids were concerned. He didn't know how it had happened. It just had. They had started dating. He had supported her during her daughter-in-law's illness and death. She had supported him through job difficulties. Now he was close to retirement and wanted to spend that retirement with her.

"Who needs a house?" he had said when Esther brought up the topic. "We can buy a motor home and see America."

"What about seeing my grandkids?"

"That's what skype is for."

"We'll talk about it," Esther had said. She wasn't ready to retire herself just yet. "Maybe when I retire, but right now, I'm needed at the center."

"Right now you are needed here," he said as he pulled her close.

Peter was happy to help Kathleen, as much as she allowed him to help. He wished she would let him do more. Once he had started dating her mother, he had passed her case on to someone else. He continued to watch over her, just in a different capacity. He had been happy to co-sign the loan for her, though he did wonder why she hadn't applied for a government loan. He decided to do some checking on her.

"My future step daughter?" he asked her current probation officer.

"Yeah, what about her?"

"She's back at school."

"I know. Good for her. She's almost done with probation."

"Is she eligible for any tuition assistance?"

"Just the student loan she took out, why?"

"So she did get the loan?"

"Sure."

"Last I talked to her it hadn't come through yet."

"She got it last month according to my records."

"That's good. Thanks, glad to know it."

"Sure thing. She really is doing well. Like I said, I don't see any reason why she won't be done with probation soon."

Peter wondered what Kathleen was using the money from the loan he had co-signed for, but decided not to confront her just yet. "Giving her a little rope," he told himself.

As happy as Esther was, she still worried about her kids. She worried about Kathleen, didn't like the fact that she was putting in so many hours and not getting paid. She had discussed it with Peter.

"There has to be a way for her to get paid. Maybe if I take out that second mortgage on the house," she said.

"You know Kathleen would never let you."

"She doesn't have to know. Besides, it's like it's her money. Her inheritance."

"Don't you think she will suspect something if you get a large influx of money?"

"What if I say Joy had an insurance policy that paid off?"

"Kathleen would know that wasn't true. She had been taking care of their accounts."

"But maybe she had one that Dale didn't know about." Peter remained silent as Esther continued to ponder possibilities. "There must be a way. What if I fiddle with the books, make it look like we are taking in more money than we are."

"You realize you're talking to a probation officer, don't you? I've got parolees that were sent up for years for doing that."

"But it's not like I'm embezzling money. I'm putting money into the account."

"It's still falsifying records."

"I see you won't be any help," Esther grunted.

"I just want to keep my future wife out of jail. Don't want to spend my honeymoon visiting you at the state penitentiary."

"Speaking of honeymoon, where are we going?" Esther changed the subject, though she had not given up.

"There must be a way," she said to herself.

Chapter 19

Esther was excited about the ballroom dancing classes she had scheduled. She proceeded to recruit couples and singles, starting with her family.

"No way, Mom," Kathleen said.

"But I want my bridal party to dance with us at the reception. You have to at least learn the waltz."

"Isn't this class for couples?" Dale asked.

"Not necessarily. Singles will be assigned a partner."

"Joy was the dancer, not me." Dale continued to protest.

"Just come for one class, see if you like it. You could dance with your sister."

This time it was Dale's turn to say, "no way!"

Finally, Kathleen was talked into it. "Okay, Mom. I'll be at the office taking care of paperwork anyway. I'll look in on the class. Won't hurt me to show some support for our new efforts."

"And I'll stop by after work if I can get someone to watch the kids."

"It's set then."

The class was about to begin when Kathleen stopped by. There were only five couples besides Peter and Esther, but Esther wasn't discouraged. Pastor Joe was there with the woman from the meeting, Ava.

"Thought that as board members we should do our best to support efforts to keep the dance studio afloat," Joe said.

The instructor called the couples out onto the dance floor and proceeded to give instructions. Kathleen was watching from the sideline.

"Oh, no," the instructor stopped. "No one watches in my class. You can be my partner," he said as he led Kathleen out on the dance floor.

"But I can't dance," Kathleen protested.

"Nonsense. There is no such thing as can't dance, just someone who hasn't learned yet."

He showed the class the steps for a simple two-step as a warm-up. "We'll save the tango for later," he said with a grin as several couples laughed encouragingly, eager to try.

"You will have a new partner by then," Kathleen informed him.

"We shall see." Part way into the dance, a cell phone rang.

"Didn't I say phones off?" The instructor stopped the lesson.

"Sorry." It was Ava's phone. "I've got to take this. It will just be a minute." She excused herself, leaving Joe without a partner.

"We can't have anyone without a partner." The instructor led Kathleen over to the space Ava had just vacated and left her.

Kathleen smiled wryly as Joe held out his hand for her to grasp. "I guess it's you and me."

"That it is," he said with a smile. At first they were so focused on learning the steps that they couldn't talk. As it got easier and the instructor turned on a simple dance tune, Kathleen relaxed enough to speak.

"I'm sorry that Scott and Stephanie aren't friends anymore."

"Are you? I thought you would be ecstatic. You didn't think my Stephanie was a good influence on your Scott."

"I thought so too, but now that it has happened, I'm not. Scott says he's all right, but I know he's not. How's Stephanie?"

"Wish I knew. She doesn't talk to me. She keeps acting out, getting into trouble. I hate to say it, but maybe your Scott is better off without my Stephanie."

"I know something about being a 'bad' girl."

"Yes, but you don't know about being the pastor's daughter, growing up in a fish bowl. All eyes on you."

"No, but I do know about growing up with only one parent. Maybe I could help." Joe pulled her to him and under his arm in a twirl. Kathleen laughed.

"Believe me, if I thought you could help, I'd be the first to call on you. And I will call on you. I just don't think she will listen to anyone right now."

Ava returned from her phone call as Dale walked into the room. It had been hard on Dale, coming inside this building. The first time since Joy's death. Only his commitment to his mother kept him from bolting.

"Oh, good. We have another couple," the instructor said as they walked in. "Come on, we are doing a two-step."

"But," Ava started, looking for Joe. When she saw him dancing with Kathleen, she gave in and took Dale's hand.

Dale stepped on her toes. "I'm sorry. I'm not a dancer. My former wife, she was the dancer."

"I know, Joy, the woman the dance studio is named after. I've heard so much about her since joining the board of directors."

"Board of directors?"

"Yes, for the dance studio, actually for the Center of the Arts. Didn't anyone tell you?"

"If they did, I probably wasn't listening. I haven't been involved in the place since my wife died."

They danced in silence for a while. Ava didn't know what to say. Finally Dale broke the silence.

""I haven't seen you running recently." He had been watching for her, hoping for another chance encounter. Ava had purposefully chosen a different time and day in order to avoid such an encounter.

"I've been running. We must be missing each other."

"When do you run? I could plan to meet you by chance."

"Oh, I never plan my runs," Ava lied. "I just fit them in when I can find the time."

"Then can you find time for coffee," he paused before adding, "With me?"

"Maybe." Ava avoided his eyes. She told herself she couldn't do this, couldn't get involved with this man, not any man but especially this man.

"Just a maybe?" He willed her to look up, unable to take his arm away from her in order to touch her chin and raise her eyes to his.

Aware of his eyes on her, she looked up and said, "More than a maybe. Call me." Dale smiled and pulled her close for a moment.

"No, no," the instructor caught the momentary embrace. "Arm's length apart. This is not a modern slow dance where you stand in place and rock back and forth. It's a two-step. You lead your partner with a gentle pressure to the back." He stepped in and took Ava away from Dale to demonstrate to the whole class.

"Now you do it." He returned Ava to her partner.

Kathleen found that Joe was not a shabby dancer.

"You've done this before," she stated.

"Not for a long time. My wife, Janice, liked to dance. She had talked me into lessons when we were first married, before the girls came along. We didn't dance much after that." Or do much of anything, he added to himself, frowning at the memory.

"Still thinking about Stephanie?" Kathleen asked.

"No, just, how time goes by, so quickly. One minute you have your whole life ahead of you, and then before you know it, it's almost half over. I used to think there would be time for dancing, once the kids were older, once the demands of parish life lessoned. That didn't happen."

"Tell me about it." Kathleen didn't want to join him in a trip down memory lane, especially memories about his wife. "At least you've done something with your life. Two kids, a parish, all the people you supposedly help at that church of yours."

"Supposedly is right. And you have two kids, too. And yours aren't in trouble. In that respect you've done more than me."

"I can't take credit for that. It's more my mom's doing. You know that."

They danced in silence for a while.

"Don't write Stephanie off just yet. She'll come around. Just look at me." Kathleen broke the silence.

"Let's hope she comes around sooner than you did," Joe commented.

"I didn't mean it that way."

"I know you didn't."

Kathleen was glad when the instructor gave them a break. No more need for small talk.

"That's my cue to leave," Kathleen said. "I was just checking out the class." She looked for Ava and found her talking with Dale, Esther and Peter.

"Kathleen, you can't leave yet," Esther said as she made her good byes. "Who will dance with Pastor Joe?"

"His dance partner," she said indicating Ava.

"But what about your brother?"

"He can find his own dance partner," Kathleen said.

"I've got to go anyway," Dale said, using the excuse to slip out the door with Kathleen. "Well, that worked out well," he said to Kathleen as they walked down the stairs to the front door.

"For you maybe, but I got stuck with that old stick-in-the mud pastor."

"You didn't seem to mind it. You looked good together."

"Believe me, it was nothing like you think. Besides he has a date, Ava."

"If so, then why did Ava give me her phone number?"

"What? Don't kid me baby brother. I can still lick you."

"Since when?"

"Since always. I know some street tricks you've never learned." Kathleen tried to put a strangle hold on Dale only to have him twist her arm behind her back.

"Ouch, I guess you have learned a few tricks of your own."

"I'm not exactly ten anymore."

"Was that how old you were when I last got one over on you?"

"About. After that I started being able to hold my own and then flip you."

"Mom always thought you were the innocent victim of my evil pranks."

"Not all the time."

"Yes, all the time. You know you were her darling. You could do no wrong."

"Only because you were so snarly and mean back then. Why was that?"

"I wish I knew, Dale. Seems so long ago. Seems I had so much anger just waiting to lash out at anyone. Mom was as good a target as any." Kathleen paused on the outside steps of the building and faced Dale. "Didn't you? Weren't you ever angry about Dad?"

"Why would I be angry?"

"Because he left us."

"It wasn't exactly his choice."

"It was his choice to work that job. He could have found a safer job."

"He liked climbing those poles," Dale said. "I have this vague memory of seeing him up on one of those poles, waving at me. He was larger than life, a giant. I was so proud."

"I don't think Mom was proud. She used to worry."

"Mom worries about everything and everyone."

"True. But weren't you ever angry at Dad, or Mom?"

"I guess Dad's death didn't affect me in the same way it did you."

"You always had the more agreeable temperament, more even." Kathleen turned and walked to the parking lot and the awaiting cars.

"And you were a spitfire, hot stuff waiting to explode, a firecracker." Dale followed after her.

"Maybe so. I still feel like I'm ready to explode at times."

"Why don't you?"

"Because I know the consequences of those explosions. Don't want to do that again." Kathleen paused as she remembered. "You never felt like you had to explode, not even when you saw other kids with their dads?"

"Grandpa was always around for me."

"Not for me."

"Guess he didn't realize you wanted him around."

"Maybe not." Kathleen didn't want to think about this anymore. She was all too aware of how unpleasant she had been. "So, you and Ava?" Kathleen gave him a friendly jab.

"It's just a phone number."

"Still this is the happiest I've seen you in a long time."

Dale didn't disagree. He climbed into his car and drove home.

Chapter 20

Joe thought about that dance and what Kathleen had said. If only she could help Stephanie. Could anyone? Stephanie balked at the mention of counselling. He had tried family counseling that first year after Janice's death. Hadn't worked. The therapist had not been a good fit, and now, Stephanie had a negative association with therapists. How like him, he thought. Whenever Janice had suggested counselling, he had refused.

"I counsel people. I don't need counseling, but if you feel you need it, go ahead," he had told her. It wasn't what she had wanted, but she had gone alone. That had been a mistake, he told himself. Too late now. By going alone the therapist only heard her side of the story. He figured she had painted him as the biggest ogre, the stereotypical church pastor who couldn't manage his marriage, who was too busy solving everyone else's problems to admit he had any of his own.

He should have gone to the sessions, then maybe he would have known what had led to her demand for a divorce. Everything was his fault, at least if he listened to her. And he did believe it for quite a while. She was the long-suffering church pastor's wife and he was the self-centered pastor who put "God and church" before his family. He had believed that for some years. Had felt guilty where his daughters were concerned, and look where that guilt had gotten him: Stephanie well on her way to a juvie home. Yes, she was like him, too much like him. Stubborn, independent, not wanting to accept help from anyone, much less from him. How could he reach her?

He had finally gone to counseling himself after Joy's death. Some of what Joy had said to him helped him realize that he was still carrying a huge burden from his wife's death. How would he be able to help Dale with his grief, or anyone, if he didn't take care of his own unresolved grief and other issues around his wife's death?

In some ways, Stephanie was like him, in other ways she was like her mother and knew just what to say to activate the guilt machine, leaving him ineffective as a parent.

One of the first things he had learned in counseling was that his wife wasn't all good, the innocent party, and he wasn't all bad.

"Try though you might to lay all the blame on your shoulders, it just doesn't belong there," Dave, his counselor had said. "And it might surprise you to know that your wife wasn't the perfect, guiltless party in your marriage. It's so easy to idealize our loved ones after they die, rather than remember their totality, including their faults and the things about them we disliked."

"Don't speak ill of the dead," Joe reminded him.

"That doesn't apply here. This is the place for honesty. If you are honest you will realize that your wife was neither all good nor all bad. She was human like you, like all of us."

Gradually Joe learned to see his wife as she was, a mixture of faults and strengths, a perfectly human being with all of her imperfections. He was helped to see his faults and strengths as well, the ways he had contributed to the problems in his marriage. And eventually he had been able to make some peace with his wife, remembering the good, forgiving the not-so-good, forgiving himself for his mistakes.

"Hopefully, if I ever marry again, I won't make the same mistakes," he had told his counselor at their last session. "I'll make other ones, new ones, not the same."

He wondered what mistakes he was making with Stephanie and Michelle that he would need to seek forgiveness for some time in the future. He hoped his daughters would find it in them to forgive him. Meanwhile he watched for any sign, any cracks in that angry façade which was Stephanie, that would allow him to get through to her.

Chapter 21

Ava had regretted giving Dale her phone number almost as soon as she had done it. She couldn't take it back now. He had been so happy, so sweet. She couldn't look him in his eyes and ask for the number back. But what right did she have to give him her phone number? What right did she have to give it to anyone, especially him? If he knew her story, he would give it back without her asking. How could she ask someone who had already suffered so much, lost his wife to cancer, to go out with someone like her? Sure, she was cancer-free now, but the former diagnosis still hung over her head, waiting to drop. Maybe not this year or the next, but sometime in the future.

And what would he think about her if he knew the rest of her history? He, whose wife had so nobly refused to abort her baby even when that baby threatened her own life? After their last encounter in the woods, Ava had asked Joe more about Dale's previous wife, Joy. He had told her how Joy had refused to even consider an abortion. And then after hearing all of those tributes to Joy at that first meeting, Ava figured Joy was a candidate for sainthood. Even if Dale were okay with her past, how could she live in the shadow of a saint? How could she compete with a saint?

Even Pastor Joe didn't know her whole story. She had told him about the divorce and the cancer, but that had left her in a positive light: The victim of a philandering husband. How little he knew about her, her true self. If he knew, would he still be her friend, him being a minister and all? Ava didn't know. What she did know was that Dale was not the guy for her, or so she told herself.

She didn't answer her phone all Saturday, hoping Dale would give up. She ran in the city streets, sloshing through piles of heavy wet snow, still better than icy paths in the woods and the possibility of running into Dale.

She came late to church, then slipped out during the closing hymn to ensure he wouldn't catch her there. How long could she keep this up, she wondered.

Dale talked to Pastor Joe at coffee hour as the crowd was thinning out.

"You know Ava," he began.

"Of course."

"You two aren't dating, are you, because she told me you weren't and gave me her phone number."

"No, we aren't dating. We're just friends."

"I've been trying to call her but she doesn't pick up. I thought maybe I'd see her at church today. Is something wrong? Do you know why she's avoiding me?"

Joe had an idea, based on what Ava had told him. "I don't know. I'll check with her and see if I can find out anything for you."

"Thanks, Pastor, I hope she's all right."

"I'll let you know."

When Ava saw Joe's familiar number come up on her cell phone, she had a pretty good idea why he was calling.

"So, you are alive."

"What are you talking about?"

"Dale said he called you all day yesterday and you never answered."

"I just didn't feel like talking."

"Is that so?"

"Yes, does a girl have to answer every time a guy calls?"

"No, but it looked to me like you were enjoying your dance with Dale Friday night." Joe hadn't been so pre-occupied with his own partner that he didn't notice that. "Dale's a fine man. I wouldn't want him to be led on."

"I'm not leading him on."

"Then why aren't you talking to him?"

"It's complicated."

"I've got all afternoon. Tell me."

"You know about my cancer."

"Yes."

"His wife died from cancer." Ava sighed as she said it. Somehow the thought of Joy's death from cancer made the possibility that it could happen to her more real.

"I know that."

"How could I put him through that again?"

"Your cancer hasn't recurred, has it?"

"No, but if it does…" When it does, she thought to herself.

"If it does, you can deal with it then. Don't you think Dale has the right to decide whether he wants to take that chance rather than you deciding for him, unless there's something else?"

"No, there's not. That's all," she bit her lower lip. These lies were becoming easier for her. They just slipped off her lips.

"So give him a call. If you don't want to go out with him, say so. If you're worried about your past bout with cancer, tell him about it and let him decide. Either way, you've got to at least talk to him."

"Okay, Joe," Ava agreed.

Shortly after she hung up, she received another phone call from Dale. She ignored the call, putting her coat on and going out to the mall.

Dale was at the mall taking Ashley and Jacob to a movie. He had tried calling Ava while waiting for Ashley to return from the restroom. No luck. They walked by the Toys R Us on their way to the car.

"Can we go inside?" Jacob begged.

"You've got plenty of toys from Christmas. You don't need anymore."

"Please, Dad," Jacob continued to beg. Ashley just looked at him.

"All right, you can look around," Dale said. They both took off. "Wait for me," Dale started to say when he saw Ava walking towards him. She saw him at the same time. Too late to pretend she didn't see him, she continued walking in his direction.

"I was beginning to think maybe you had given me the wrong number or had changed your mind about coffee."

"Sorry, just a little under the weather yesterday. I didn't answer my phone all day."

"So how about that coffee?"

Ava paused. This wasn't exactly the ideal place to talk.

"Is something wrong?" Dale asked, watching for Jacob and Ashley.

"No, coffee would be good," she finally said. They set a date for next Saturday before Ashley came out of the store, looking for him.

"Come on, Dad," she said, not looking at Ava. Jacob followed her out.

"Hi, Miss Ava," Jacob came running and gave Ava a big hug.

"I see you know Jacob," Dale said with a grin.

"That I do, and Ashley as well." Ava smiled. "How are you, Ashley?"

Ashley ignored her, pulling on her dad's arm. "Come on, Dad. You said you would come with us."

"Ashley, I think Miss Ava spoke to you. You're being rude."

"I'm fine," Ashley muttered. "Now can we go, Dad?"

"Just a minute," he instructed. "Go back in the store. I'll be right there." Ashley went part way then hung by the store opening, waiting for her dad.

"I'm sorry about that," Dale apologized for Ashley's behavior.

"Don't worry about it. I wouldn't want to share my dad with someone else either. Go on, Ashley's waiting for you." Ava dismissed him with a smile.

"What harm is a cup of coffee?" she told herself.

"I don't like Miss Ava," Ashley commented that night over supper.

"What brought that on," Dale asked.

"Nothing. I just don't like her."

"You don't have to like her."

"I like her," Jacob chimed in. "She's pretty."

"Why don't you like her?" Dale asked Ashley.

"I just don't. She's bossy." Ashley fidgeted in her seat, playing with her food, avoiding her father's gaze.

"When was she bossy?"

"When we had practice for the Christmas pageant. She bossed everyone around."

"I think that's what directors do, Ashley."

"I don't care, I still don't like her." Ashley put her fork down. "Can I go now?"

"Well, I do – like her that is. And yes, you can go."

"I like her, too," Jacob agreed. "Can I have ice cream?"

Chapter 22

"Dad, is it all right if I take Irish Dance lessons? I'll pay for it with my baby sitting money," Michelle asked Joe. "I can take the bus after school and do homework until class starts. All you'll have to do is pick me up."

"I didn't know you were interested in dance lessons. You never said anything about it before."

"It's just that I know it's expensive and all."

"Nothing we couldn't work out."

"So is it okay?"

"Sure. When do they start?" Michelle and Stephanie had taken dance lessons before, but that had been Janice's doing. She had set them up, taken the girls to class and paid for them with the money she had made from her part-time job. After her death, the girls had not said anything about wanting to continue so he hadn't pursued it. Stephanie had seemed to be thankful not to go. It had not occurred to him that Michelle wanted to take lessons.

Kathleen stood with the parents watching the first class. Aware of the audience, Patrick put on a show. He had brought his daughter to demonstrate what the students would be learning.

"They have to know what they are working towards or they won't be willing to do the work." He stood by Kathleen as his daughter danced, kicking her legs high and sliding across the floor with her arms tight to her side.

"Okay, everyone." He turned off the music and addressed the class. "Eventually, if you work hard, you will be able to dance like Caitlin here. How many years have you been dancing, Caitlin?"

"Four."

"Wow," Ashley thought. "She looks like she's my age. She must have started dancing when she was five."

"You won't be able to dance like Caitlin your first year, but if you work at it, you will over time. We'll start with soft shoes and wait for hard shoes."

"Is it like toe shoes in ballet?" Ashley asked.

"No. It's not the same. Hard shoes are more like tap shoes. You wear different shoes based on the dance. Soft shoes, or ghillies, are worn for jigs and reels. Hard shoes are for the hornpipe. We're going to start with some simple jigs and reels," Patrick explained. "Maybe next year we'll try a hornpipe."

Ashley was still taking ballet lessons, but had to wait a couple more years before graduating to toe shoes. She didn't want to wait that long for these shoes.

"And, if you do well this year, there are competitions in Detroit every spring. Some of you might be able to compete in the beginning level." Ashley smiled at this. She was tired of repeated lessons and only a recital to show for it.

"Let's get started," Patrick said. Kathleen checked on the other classes, talking to parents she had come to know over the course of the past year, answering questions, problem solving. She returned to the Irish dance class as it was getting close to ending to see how it had gone.

A larger crowd of parents were gathered as those who had stayed for the whole lesson were joined by those who had come to pick up their children. She saw Pastor Joe among them.

"I saw that Michelle had signed up for these classes? Another way to support the Center? Not that I'm complaining."

"It was all her idea. She's even using her babysitting money to pay for it."

"She's a good sitter. Ashley and Jacob love her."

"And she loves them." Kathleen looked around.

"No Ava today?"

"No, why would she be here?"

"Just seems like every time I see you lately you've been together."

"Why don't you like Ava? She could really use some friends."

"I thought that was what she had you for."

"Female friends. It's hard, moving to a new city where you don't know anyone. It's hard to make friends. You should know that. It hasn't been too long since you were a newcomer. At least you had family." That she did. Kathleen didn't know what she would have done without her family. She definitely wouldn't be here. "Besides, with her theater background, maybe she could help with the recital."

"Okay. I'll mention it to Leticia. And I'll try to be more friendly. Is that your job, trying to get everyone to get along?"

"Part of it," Joe smiled. Patrick had his students sit on the floor as he turned on some music. This time he danced with his daughter for the class. The parents clapped when they finished.

"Just a reminder of what you are working toward," he said to his class. He then addressed the parents. "And you don't have to be young to learn. Anyone can learn. I could offer a class for adults if any of you are interested." Kathleen looked around her to assess interest. She saw some smiles but no clear "yes."

"If you are interested, just let Kathleen know, and we'll see what can be worked out." Patrick pointed to Kathleen. He then talked to his class about dance shoes and music for practice at home. He gave them handouts with the steps they had learned that day and, before dismissing the class, told them to practice.

Michelle joined her dad and Kathleen. "Dad, I need to get shoes." She was flushed and smiling, clearly having enjoyed the class.

"Where do we get them?" Joe asked Kathleen. "Do you have any?"

"Not yet, but I will," Kathleen told him.

As the room cleared of parents and students, Kathleen approached Patrick while he was changing his shoes.

"Thanks for the heads up," she said, her voice expressing her displeasure.

"What do you mean?"

"You neglected to tell me that special shoes were required."

"Oh, I did. I guess you know now. You didn't do your homework before setting up this class, did you?"

"I thought that was what I had you for. So how do I get shoes for the class?"

"How about we talk about it over dinner?" Ashley and Jacob approached Kathleen. "Looks like your daughter is about the same age as my daughter. We could go to McDonald's or get pizza."

"This isn't my daughter. It's my niece, Ashley, and my nephew Jacob." Kathleen introduced them.

"And why aren't you taking my class, young man? We could use more men," Patrick asked Jacob.

"Can I, Aunt Kathleen?" Jacob asked.

"It's up to you, just check with your dad first," Kathleen answered.

"So, how about dinner?" Patrick asked.

"I have to take the kids home, but maybe it wouldn't hurt to get something to eat first. I'll call their grandma. But please, no McDonald's or Pizza Hut." Kathleen had had enough of them while working there two years ago. "I don't care if I ever eat at either of them again. There's plenty of other pizza places."

"Your pick. You know the area. My treat."

Mary was watching Grace. She had a meal prepared so she was not happy about the change of plans.

"It will still taste good tomorrow," Kathleen had insisted as Mary sputtered. Ashley and Jacob were happy. They never missed an opportunity for pizza.

The kids sat in a separate booth, eating their pepperoni pizza, so Kathleen and Patrick could talk over a supreme pizza.

"Do you think there is enough interest for an adult class?" Kathleen asked.

"As long as I'm driving this far, I might as well make it worth my time by teaching a second class."

"I know, but is there interest? No one approached me about it."

"Give it some time. As word gets out we might have enough for a class. How about you? Wouldn't you like to learn?"

Kathleen laughed. "I'm no dancer. I can 'free-style' with the best of them, but Irish dance ..."

"You don't know until you try. You just may like it. And if you sign up, others will follow."

"Is that so?"

"You're a natural leader, Kathleen. Kathleen is such a pretty Irish name. Are you sure you're not Irish?" Kathleen smiled at his Irish brogue.

"Is that what you Irish call blarney?"

"It's only blarney if it's not true."

"And what about those shoes? How do I get them before the next class?" Kathleen got back to business.

At the end of the next class, Patrick pulled Kathleen out from the group of watching parents.

"Anyone can learn," he said. "You're never too old. Come on, Kathleen. Anyone else want to try?" A few mothers came forward, joining Kathleen on the dance floor as Patrick taught them a simple step while their children watched.

"Now that wasn't so bad, was it?" Patrick said as they finished. "This is just a taste. If you want to learn more, I'll be teaching a class for adults if I can get a minimum of six students."

"Kathleen, are you signed up?" one parent asked.

"She's my first student," Patrick answered for her. "How many more are interested?" There was a show of hands, not a lot, but more than six, enough to make a class possible. Joe had watched along with the other parents. He didn't know what it was, but he didn't like this guy. Kathleen took names of those interested and signed them up.

"How about you, Pastor?" she asked Joe.

"Not for me."

"So, Kathleen," Patrick joined them. "How about dinner again?"

"Mary will kill me if I keep ruining her home-cooked meals with pizza."

"So we drop the kids off at their home and you and I go. My daughter is with her mom."

"Hard to say no to that," Kathleen agreed. Joe put his arm around Michelle's shoulder and led her out, the hair on his neck bristling as he did.

"There's something about that guy I just don't like," he muttered as he watched Patrick escort Kathleen out of the building.

Chapter 23

All week Dale looked forward to having coffee with Ava. The plan was to meet at three. That way, if all goes well, they would have dinner. If it didn't go well, they hadn't expended that much time and could go their separate ways. Dale was counting on dinner. He had Esther lined up to watch the kids for him.

"What are we doing Saturday night?" Peter asked Esther.

"That depends."

"On what?"

"On whether Dale's date for coffee goes well. If it goes well, you'll be helping me babysit."

"Finally, Dale is doing something for himself," Peter said. "I hope it goes well."

Dale was early, arriving by quarter to three, tapping his foot as he waited. He jumped up as he saw Ava approach, asked what kind of coffee she wanted and pulled out a chair for her.

"A gentleman," Ava smiled. "Caramel Machiata."

Dale couldn't keep himself from staring at her as she tasted the frothy drink. He liked the way her hair framed her face, short and pixie like. So different from Joy who had always had long hair that she tied up into a bun, at least until the chemo treatments. He had to stop comparing Ava to Joy, he told himself as the thoughts kept coming unbidden.

"So, tell me about yourself. You already know about my former wife. What about you? Any relationships? What brought you here?"

"I was married. Not much to tell. It didn't work out. I wanted a clean slate, wanted to move away from all I knew and all who knew me. I heard about the position at St. Luke's through my pastor, applied and here I am."

"Here you are," Dale said with a smile. "You said there was something you wanted to tell me?"

Ava hesitated. She didn't want to go through with telling him about her past. She had rehearsed what she would say all week, but now that the time was here ... Did she really want to tell him? She took a deep breath.

"Well, it's not quite as simple as I stated." Dale waited, giving Ava time to gather her thoughts.

"It wasn't just because of the divorce that I moved here. I had uterine cancer." No need for the details, she told herself. He didn't need to know about Edward's philandering. Plenty of time for that if this relationship lasts beyond today. Dale continued to wait patiently. "They caught it early. I had a hysterectomy. The prognosis is good. I have a clean bill of health."

"Then, that's good," Dale said.

"Yes, but, you know how it is with cancer. There's always the possibility of a recurrence."

Dale definitely knew about that. He wasn't sure how he felt. "So how long have you been cancer free?"

"Two years."

"That's good." Joy hadn't made it that long, he added to himself.

"I understand if you don't want to see me, after all you have already gone through."

Dale wasn't sure what to say. He had known that Ava had something to tell him. He had thought it would be about former relationships, not cancer. She appeared so young and healthy, just like Joy had before her diagnosis. For some reason the information wasn't registering. He wasn't sure what he thought.

"Do you want me to leave?" Ava asked.

"No, er, I don't know," he responded. "No, stay." He took her hand across the table. They were both startled when his phone rang. Dale checked to see who the caller was. His mom.

"Sorry, I've got to take this," he said as he answered.

"Dale, Jacob has fallen."

"What?" Dale asked. For a moment he thought she had said Joy had fallen, like that phone call over two years ago.

"Jacob has fallen, off the trampoline. Or actually, Ashley pushed him. I'm sorry. I thought it would be okay to let them play with the neighbor kids," Esther said in a rush of words. They didn't make any sense to Dale.

"Is he all right?"

"Yes, we think so. The neighbors called an ambulance just to make sure. They think he may have broken his arm."

"Where are you?"

"At the emergency room. Ashley and Grace are with me. We followed the ambulance. Don't worry. You don't need to rush. They came at normal speed. They didn't want to take any chances because Jacob passed out at first."

"I'll be right there."

"Don't rush," Esther said. Would she always have to be the bearer of bad news for her son? She, too, had flashbacked to that phone call over two years ago when Joy had fallen at the dance studio. This was a different situation; still, it stirred feelings of dread.

"What's wrong?" Ava asked, trying to piece together what had happened from the one-sided conversation she had heard.

"Jacob. Seems he fell off the neighbor's trampoline and broke his arm. He's at the emergency room. I've got to go."

"Do you want me to come with you?"

"No, it may take a while. There's no reason for you to spend your whole night at the hospital."

"At least let me drive myself to the hospital. I want to know how Jacob is too."

"Okay." Dale wasn't up to arguing. He kept remembering that phone call when Joy had fallen and all that had ensued. He assured himself that this was different but he couldn't shake the feeling that something terrible was about to happen.

He greeted Esther and his children in the emergency waiting room. Grace ran to meet him and jumped into his arms. The feeling of déjà vu permeated the room as he remembered waiting with his mom to see Joy.

"He's back there but they won't let the kids come back with me."

Ava had hung back, not wanting to intrude. At this, she came forward.

"I can stay with Ashley and Grace so you can go back and see Jacob," she offered.

Ashley gave her a look that said, "What are you doing here?" but Ava held her own.

"Thank you, Ava. That would help." Dale handed Grace over to her.

"Come on." Ava put Grace down and took her hand. "Maybe we can find some toys. Ashley, are you coming?"

"I'm not going anywhere. I want to see Jacob."

"You can't see Jacob right now. We'll see if you can later. Right now, stay with Miss Ava, okay?" Dale told her.

Ava offered Ashley her other hand. Ashley refused to take it but she followed Ava. Ava and Dale exchanged glances before he went through the double doors into the emergency room.

Jacob was in good spirits. The paramedics had given him a stuffed animal, a lion.

"Just like Aslan," Jacob said, showing his Dad. "He's here to protect me." Joy had loved *The Chronicles of Narnia* and used to read them out-loud at night to Ashley and Jacob. Aslan, the lion, was the God figure in the books.

"That's great," Dale said as he approached. Jacob's arm was splinted and in a sling.

"The paramedics had splinted his arm to keep him for moving it," Esther told him, following his gaze.

"Does it hurt much?" Dale asked.

"Not as much as at first," Jacob responded.

"That's my brave boy." Dale gave him a careful hug. A nurse came in and took his temperature and blood pressure.

"Are you the father?" she asked.

"Yes," he said as if admitting guilt. Why did he feel so guilty? Why was it every time you brought a child into the emergency room, you were looked at as if you were the worst sort of criminal and had been abusing your child?

"What happened?" the nurse asked.

"He wasn't there when it happened," Esther spoke up. "I was. It happened on my watch." Esther rushed to her son's defense.

"It says here, trampoline incident."

"Yes, he fell off the neighbor's trampoline," Esther said.

"Weren't there any spotters?"

"No, I guess not. I didn't see it happen. All I know is what the neighbors told me," Esther explained.

"Hmmmmm," the nurse made some notations. "I'm afraid it will be a while before we can get x-rays. There are a number of more serious cases ahead of you." At this she exited the room.

"What were the kids doing on the trampoline anyway?" An accusatory note crept into Dale's voice. They had had some unseasonably warm weather resulting in an early thaw, making the trampoline an irresistible attraction.

"They told me they were going to the neighbors. I thought they would be okay. I guess the lure of the trampoline was too great. I didn't even realize the trampoline was still up in their backyard." Dale didn't respond. He didn't want to take his anger out on his mom. Now that he knew Jacob was okay, the feelings he had suppressed pushed to the surface.

"Addy had been outside watching them when it happened. It seems Jacob wanted to jump with Ashley and Sabrina. Ashley told him to get off and when he didn't, she pushed him hard enough that he fell."

Dale could see the scenario unfold in his mind's eye. Ashley had been a problem lately, always angry. She had been getting into trouble at school for fighting on the playground. Dale hadn't known what to do. Last year when he had expected the kids to act out, they hadn't. Ashley had been better behaved than she had ever been before, much to his surprise. He didn't know where this new found anger was coming from.

"It may be a long wait, Mom. Why don't you take the kids home? There's no reason for all of us to wait here."

"This must be the place." They were interrupted by a familiar voice as Peter poked his head into the room. "They weren't going to let me back here, but I still have some pull. Told them I was Jacob's grandfather. That's right, isn't it, Jacob?" He smiled at Jacob. "How you doing?"

Jacob smiled, enjoying the attention.

"Look who else I found." Ashley stepped out from behind Peter. "She wanted to know how her brother was doing."

Ashley stepped forward, carrying a Monster Truck book and a coloring book with crayons as peace offerings.

"Miss Ava bought these for you." Ashley gave them to her brother then retreated to Peter's side.

"Is there anything else you want to say to your brother?" Dale asked her.

"I'm sorry for pushing you," Ashley said, clinging to Peter for safety.

"That's okay." Jacob was not one to hold a grudge. His memory was short. Ashley left Peter's side long enough to give Jacob a hug.

"What's going on in here?" the nurse appeared. "We can't have this many people in a room. Some of you have to leave."

"That'll be me and Ashley," Peter volunteered.

"I better relieve Ava of Grace," Esther added. "I'll take the kids home," she told Dale. "Let me know if anything else happens."

"I will," Dale reassured his mom. "And I'll deal with you, young lady, when I get home," he told Ashley before she could slip out of the room with Peter.

Ava had managed to distract Ashley by taking her and Grace to the hospital gift shop where she had picked out the gifts for Jacob.

"He likes Monster Trucks," Ashley had said as she looked through the assortment of children's books.

"So we'll get him that. What about a coloring book?" They had agreed on a Super Hero coloring book. Peter had arrived when they returned to the waiting room.

"I want to see Jacob," Ashley insisted.

"We'll see what we can do about that," Peter had said, leaving Ava with Grace who was playing with the stuffed animal Ava had bought her from the gift shop.

After Peter and Esther left with the kids, Ava joined Dale and Jacob. Peter gave Esther a knowing smile as he nodded in Ava's direction. "The date?" he asked. Esther smiled back, too busy with Ashley and Grace to respond further.

"Miss Ava," Jacob said. "Look what Ashley gave me." He held up the Monster Truck book.

Dale smiled at her. "I believe Miss Ava had something to do with that."

"Ashley picked them out," Ava responded.

"Atonement," Dale said. "Did you know Ashley was the one who pushed Jacob off the trampoline?"

"No, hadn't heard that." She had heard about Ashley getting into fights on the playground though. It was a small school.

"She's trouble," she had heard another teacher say during her break in the teacher's lounge, referring to Ashley. "Last week she pushed Carly down. This week she picked a fight with Jimmy Roberts." Ava hadn't said anything. She had made a point of watching for Ashley during recess and lunch break to observe her behavior. Any attempt she made to talk to Ashley was rebuffed.

"Time for you to go for a ride." An orderly came in with a wheel chair. "Time for x-rays. Hop in," he said to Jacob. "We'll be back shortly. Are you the parents?"

"I'm his dad."

"Did you want to come along?"

"Sure," Dale said, looking first at Ava.

"Go ahead. You stay with him. Do you want me to wait for you?"

"No, go on home. Who knows how long it will be before we get the results from the x-rays. Us guys will hang out, right Jacob?" he nodded at Jacob. "And thanks for the books," he told her as he followed Jacob out the door.

Dale had been relieved to have Ava go. Much as he appreciated her help, he wasn't sure about what she had told him. He hadn't fully comprehended at first, felt numb. Now it seemed all of the pain of those years dealing with Joy's cancer had come flooding back. Memories of visits to the hospital, the emergency room. He didn't think he could go through that again.

Chapter 24

Ashley was subdued the rest of the night. She helped with Grace and didn't fuss when Esther told her it was time to get ready for bed.

"When will Jacob come home?" she asked as she brushed her teeth.

"Soon. Your dad said they were just waiting to talk to the doctor."

"Can't I wait for Jacob?"

"We don't know when that will be." Esther was surprised when Ashley didn't put up a fight.

"Not like her," she thought. Ashley had been so quiet that first year after her mother's death. Instead of acting out, she had been helpful around the house, helping with both Grace and Jacob. What had happened to that little girl so full of life? Esther had actually been relieved when Ashley had started fighting with her brother again. A sign that she was starting to heal, Esther had thought. She wished she knew what was going on in that small head, much as she had wondered about Kathleen over thirty years ago. Joy's death had brought back the pain of those years after her husband's death. Sure it was different. The death of a mother is different from the death of a father, but not that different. Dale had had time to prepare for the loss, whereas she had been taken unaware. He seemed to be handling it okay, though he did work a lot. And now, just maybe there was someone else in his life, someone to take his mind off of Joy and off of work. She wanted him to have the happiness she was finding with Peter.

Esther tucked Ashley into bed.

"Grandma, why doesn't Daddy love me anymore?"

"What? What are you talking about, Ashley? Of course your dad loves you."

"But he hardly ever does anything with us anymore."

"He took you to the movies last week," Esther defended her son.

"That was just one time. He's always working. He doesn't play with us the way he used to. And when he is home, he's so sad. I try to be good but he's still sad."

"He misses your mom," Esther explained.

"I miss her too, but why doesn't he love me?"

"Honey, all I can say is that your dad loves you very, very much. Do you believe me?"

"No."

"But he does," Esther hugged her and kissed her on the forehead. "Now go to sleep."

Peter had settled onto the couch, watching basketball when Esther came back downstairs.

"The kids settled?" he asked as she slipped in next to him.

"Yes," Esther sighed. "Ashley wanted to know why her dad doesn't love her anymore."

"What did you say?"

"What could I say? I told her he loved her."

"Do you think she believed you?"

"No. Dale has been gone a lot, working late. But Jacob seems to be okay."

"Different kids react differently to loss. I'm sure Kathleen reacted differently from Dale when their dad died."

"Did she ever. Kathleen had a chip on her shoulder she dared anyone to knock off."

"And Dale?"

"He was like Jacob. Didn't let it bother him, at least not as far as I could see."

"Sometimes after the death of a spouse, the remaining spouse is so engulfed in grief that they forget that the children are grieving too. It's like the children lose both parents." Peter slipped into counseling mode, carefully proceeding. "Was that the case for you?"

"It's so long ago. I don't know. I do know I had so much work to do, taking care of the kids and then getting a job to support them. My parents helped as much as they could, but there was still so much to do. I didn't have anyone taking care of my kids the way Dale does. I couldn't bury myself in work, even if I had wanted to. Besides, the kids kept me rooted. I think without them, I truly would have gone crazy with grief. I couldn't fall apart because my kids were counting on me." Peter hugged her close to him.

"You think I should tell Dale what Ashley said? He's already got so much to deal with."

"I'd want to know if it were my daughter. We men, sometimes we have to be forced to see what is right before our eyes. We aren't as tuned in to the feelings of those around us as women are."

"It is a skill that can be learned," Esther said with a smile.

"Are you offering to teach me?"

"Are you willing to learn?" Esther gave him a kiss. They heard the back door open as Jacob came through the door and ran into the living room to show them his cast.

"Broken?" Peter asked as Dale came in.

"Yep, a nice clean break though. He will heal. Kids heal quickly." Dale turned to Jacob. "Get ready for bed. I'll be up shortly."

"Can I show my cast to Ashley?"

"No, let her sleep. You can show her tomorrow."

"Okay," Jacob reluctantly went up the stairs.

"Time for me to leave, too," Peter said, giving Esther a chance to talk with her son alone.

"Any problems with Grace and Ashley?" Dale asked.

"No, they were good, except ..."

"Except what?" Dale prepared himself. "What has Ashley done now?"

"She hasn't done anything," Esther started, buying herself time as she chose her words. Dale looked so tired. She hated to burden him further. "She asked me why you don't love her anymore."

"What?"

"That's what she said. Why doesn't Daddy love me anymore?"

"Where did she get that idea?"

"You have been working a lot of hours."

"I took her and Jacob to the movies just last week," he defended himself.

"I'm just telling you what she said."

"Someone has to keep a roof over our heads. I'm still paying off Joy's medical bills."

"I know. You've been working very hard. Maybe too hard. You don't play with the kids the way you used to."

"Maybe I don't feel like playing. Maybe I'm too tired to play." Dale turned away from her.

"Look, Dale, I know it's hard. But you've got a daughter upstairs who misses you. Isn't it enough that she lost her mother? Does she have to lose her father as well?" Dale felt uncharacteristic anger swelling within him. He turned back to face his mother.

"What do you know about it, Mom?"

"I know what it is to lose a spouse."

"But it's not the same."

"No, no two griefs are alike."

"I enter the house and all I see is Joy. I look at my children and I see their mother and all I no longer have. And just when I think I might have found someone else, I am reminded of all I lost." Dale fought the urge to strike out, turning away again.

"You've lost a lot, but your children have too. Can't you see that Ashley needs you?" Esther put her hand on his shoulder.

"I can't do this right now, Mom," Dale pulled away. "I'll call you tomorrow."

"See you at church?"

"Yeah, sure, at church."

"Daddy," Jacob called. "I need help."

"I'll be right there." Dale went upstairs while Esther let herself out.

Jacob had his shirt half-way off. He wasn't able to pull it off over his cast without help. Dale helped him put on his pajamas and brush his teeth.

"Luckily you are left-handed," Dale said as Jacob brushed. "It would be a lot harder if you had broken your left arm instead of your right."

"Are you sure I can't show Ashley my cast?"

Ashley appeared in the bathroom. "Ashley, look," Jacob showed off the cast. "See, the doctor signed it."

"You'll be the hit of the playground on Monday," Dale commented. "What are you doing up?" he asked Ashley.

"I heard Jacob."

"Okay, now to bed, both of you." Dale tucked in Jacob first then went to Ashley's room. Grace was sound asleep in her bed.

Dale tucked Ashley in. "Grandma said you were asking why I didn't love you anymore."

Ashley didn't respond.

"You know I love you, very much," Dale continued.

"But you're never home. And you don't play with us."

"I've been working a lot, that doesn't mean I don't love you. I have to make money to pay the bills."

"You can have my allowance."

"Thank you, baby, but that's not necessary."

"But if you need money …"

"You know, I'll try to be better. I have been gone a lot. How about we spend all day together tomorrow, after church?"

"You don't have to work?"

"It's Sunday, not a work day."

"You won't be too tired?"

"Never too tired for my girl. Now go to sleep. I love you." He kissed her on her forehead.

"I love you too, Daddy," Ashley responded. Dale sighed as he walked back downstairs, his shoulders drooping as if carrying a heavy burden.

Jacob was the center of attention at church that morning. Everyone wanted to hear what had happened.

When Jacob proudly said, "Ashley pushed me," Dale could see the eyes of the older church women say how that girl needed a mother. He hoped they wouldn't renew their efforts to find him a wife.

"How are you, Jacob?" Ava asked after church. Ashley grabbed Dale by the hand.

"Come on, Dad. You promised."

"I told Ashley I would spend the day with her," Dale explained to Ava. He found himself avoiding Ava's eyes. He wasn't sure what he thought at that point.

"That's good," Ava said, smiling at Ashley. "I'm glad Jacob is okay," she said to Dale before leaving. She didn't say anything about calling. She figured it was up to him whether he wanted to pursue a relationship or not. Still she felt a pang of sadness.

"Who was she to deserve happiness?" she reminded herself.

Chapter 25

Kathleen was enjoying the attention of not just Patrick, the Irish charmer, but of Jerome, Letty's cousin. Her excursions into the neighboring city had been curtailed because of her classes and the need to study, not to mention her finances. Still she tried to get to Delbert's club once or twice a month on Saturday night, whenever Letty was going. Delbert liked her and treated her to dinner. She had shared her business problems with him. It was nice to have someone removed from the situation, someone who wasn't family or going to be family, to talk to.

Jerome usually joined them at their table in between his responsibilities at the bar. As manager he made the rounds, greeted people, checked on whether they were receiving the service they expected, also checked on people that might need to be removed. He was trouble shooting, while his dad entertained friends. He also managed the entertainment. He always made a point of ending up at her table as the night wore on.

"I don't know what your dad was talking about, saying you weren't able to run the place," Kathleen told him.

"No one can run the place as far as he's concerned, except for him."

"He actually offered me a position that first night I was here."

"All talk. He'd like some white candy in his bar. Thinks maybe he'll attract more white business that way. I say we're fine the way we are. We don't need no white traffic in here. Only causes trouble."

"Oh?" Kathleen raised her eyebrows.

"You're okay. You fit in all right. But we don't want to get too white."

"So is that what I am? White candy?" Kathleen asked with a smile. "Not sure I like that."

Delbert walked up and asked, "What kinds of nonsense are you talking about, son?"

"He said he didn't want the place to get too white, but I'm okay."

"White money is as good as black money. It's all green to me," Delbert responded.

Letty spent the night on the dance floor. When Jerome had a break he would dance with Kathleen. Other times he would join the band for a number or two. At times a rap session would break out, especially when Letty's cousin Douglas was home from Chicago for the weekend. Sometimes he would bring his friend Omar. When he did, he and Letty danced together all night. He was her favorite dance partner.

"The two of you belong on 'So You Think You Can Dance'," her uncle told her.

"You arrange it, Uncle Delbert," Letty laughed.

Jerome was not a shabby dancer either.

"You black folk are born with rhythm," Kathleen teased as they rocked to the beat.

"Just shut up and feel the music," Jerome told her, placing his hands on her hips and helping her move with him. Kathleen liked Jerome, but resisted his charms. He was definitely a ladies man. Kathleen watched him flirt with different women in the bar.

"It's just business," he told her. "Make them feel wanted, and they want to come back."

"Is that so? Is that what you are doing with me?" Kathleen didn't wait for an answer as she took a sip of her drink. She figured it was better if they remained friends.

"What about you and me?" Jerome asked.

"Just business," Kathleen said. "Good company and drinks," she added.

That's where Kathleen had been the night of Jacob's accident. She had been on her way to pick up Letty when Esther had called.

"He's fine. It's probably no worse than a broken arm. You don't have to come to the hospital," Esther had told her. Kathleen had been grateful for that. She had been studying all day for an exam on Monday and wanted to let off a little steam.

She came over to check on Jacob the next afternoon.

"Aunt Kathleen, want to sign my cast?" Jacob came running.

"Doesn't seem to have slowed him down any," Kathleen commented to Dale.

"Nothing slows him down," Dale responded. "He's just one of those happy kids." Kathleen envied him.

"Did you go to the ballroom dance class this Friday?" Dale asked.

"No, and apparently you didn't either."

"It's not for me. Mom's on a war path though. She's determined to get us there."

"How about a pact? I won't go if you don't go," Kathleen suggested.

"Pinky swear," Dale agreed as they wrapped their pinkies together. It felt good to gang up against their mom like they had done as kids, before Kathleen became too wild and Dale too much of a stuffed shirt in her mind.

They were interrupted by the doorbell and the entrance of Pastor Joe and Michelle.

"Sorry to intrude, but Michelle wanted to see how Jacob was doing. She brought him some of her home-made cookies," Joe said.

"Didn't she see him at church," Ashley said.

"Ashley, don't be rude," Dale scolded. Ashley stomped off upstairs. "I'm sorry. I promised I'd spend the day with her," Dale explained.

"We're the ones who need to apologize, we showed up without calling."

"You're always welcome, Pastor."

"Well, I suggest you go talk to that daughter of yours. We can let ourselves out."

"No need to leave. You can hang out with Kathleen for a while," Dale suggested.

Jacob was showing his loot to Michelle. "It's like Christmas, or my birthday," he said, pointing out the gifts that were accumulating.

"Well don't be getting any idea about making this a regular event," Kathleen said to Jacob. "Again no Ava," she turned to Joe. "This is getting to be a habit."

"Ava saw Jacob at church."

"Oh … you want something to drink?" Kathleen didn't know how to be a good hostess. She usually relied on her mother for such conventions, but Esther was spending the day with Peter and his mom.

"No, we'll be going soon." They stood awkwardly, neither making a move to leave.

"So, you going to take Irish dance lessons?" Joe asked.

"Haven't quite decided. That was just to get others to sign-up."

"A ruse, huh?"

"If anyone can get the ladies to sign up, Patrick can. He's a charmer."

"Oh," Joe didn't know what to say to that. "You weren't at the ballroom dance classes on Friday?"

"No, I only went that first time to see how it was going. I like to check on new classes, make sure the instructors have everything they need." Again an awkward silence. This time it was Kathleen's turn to break the silence.

"Stephanie didn't want to come?"

"No, she isn't exactly into doing anything as a family, especially not visiting church members."

"So, is that what we are to you? Church members?" Joe didn't know how to respond to this question. It was always tricky, these boundary issues. When did church members cross the line to become friends?

"You aren't," he finally said.

"And not going to be."

"I don't expect you to." Joe looked at his watch. "Michelle, I think it's time we leave. We've taken up enough of their time."

"Don't leave. We can play a game," Jacob interceded.

"That's okay, bud. We can play some other time," Michelle told him as they left. Kathleen escorted them, holding the door as they said goodbye.

"Well, that was awkward," Joe stated.

"What was?" Michelle asked.

"Nothing, Michelle, nothing that concerns you," he said, climbing into the car.

"Why do all these people have to come to our house?" Ashley asked.

"It's just your Aunt Kathleen and Michelle. You like them."

"And Pastor Joe."

"Don't you like Pastor Joe?"

"I thought we were going to spend time together."

"We are, we will."

"When?"

"Isn't that what we are doing right now?"

"No." Ashley turned over in her bed, her back to him.

"Then what do you want to do?" She rolled back over in response.

"Can we play a game, just you and me and Jacob? The way we used to?"

"I can manage that," Dale agreed. "How about we play Candyland so Grace can play too?"

"Okay."

"Now come on downstairs. You're still not too big for me to carry." He tickled her till she laughed, then picked her up and threw her over his shoulder and carried her downstairs.

No heavier than Joy was that last month, he thought to himself.

Chapter 26

Twice blessed, that they were. Now that Sara knew why she was blowing up so fast, she was relieved. But she had to plan for two babies, two cribs, double the clothes, double the diapers. The thought of one baby had been overwhelming enough. But two.

"One is in front of the other, that's why I only heard one heart beat," the midwife had told her when the ultrasound revealed two small fetuses. Sara and Larry remained firm in not wanting to know the gender of the babies.

"Though sometimes I think I have Jacob and Esau wrestling inside me," Sara said, referring to biblical twins.

Sara loved having Letty stay over those weekends she had her dance workshops. The only problem Sara had with it was that she didn't get to see enough of her. The weekends were intense. The workshop ran from six to ten on Friday, nine to five on Saturday, and ten to two on Sunday. Letty arrived around eleven on Friday and was gone by eight on Saturday. The only real time they had with her was on Saturday night and sometimes not even that time as Letty went out with friends from her class.

Sara loved hearing about Joy's Dance School and the progress on "The Center," as they referred to the Center for Healing and the Arts. She wanted to know what was happening and catch up on news from home. She called her mom every week, but it wasn't the same as being there. When Joy had been alive, she had called several times a week. It was different now that Joy was gone. She had no one to call but her mom and her mom didn't always have the information Sara longed to hear. She missed the close connection to her nieces and nephew and Dale and his family members, Esther and Kathleen. It seemed Joy had been the link that kept them together. Without her she had not only lost her sister, but all those other connections she had through her sister. At least that was how it felt. Dale, Esther and Kathleen were always cordial when she visited, but she felt like an outsider in their family circle.

Sara loved Larry and their new home, but sometimes it seemed like she rattled around in this mammoth old house. It was way too big for just the two of them. Another reason she was glad for Letty. Anne, her college roommate, was renting the small apartment over their garage. The extra money was nice, but the company was even better. Many nights Larry worked late, leaving her alone to ramble around with her thoughts. Those days she especially enjoyed Anne's company.

She liked Detroit, but still, it was Detroit. Even though they were in a relatively safe neighborhood and had a neighborhood watch, there was still reason for concern about safety, especially with not just one but two babies coming.

"How about we get a dog? A big dog. I mean, he would be our best security system," Larry had suggested.

"How about an alarm system? You don't have to clean up after an alarm system or take them for walks," Sara countered.

"A dog will be good company, especially when I'm not home at night." They had compromised and gotten both. Larry cursed when he came home at night and accidentally set off the alarm system. Or when he went outside to take out the garbage in the morning and woke up the neighbors with the alarm, but Sara felt better knowing they would be alerted if anyone tried to break in.

"I mean, they won't be able to slaughter us in our sleep," she told Larry.

Larry shook his head. "A dog will alert us, too."

"But we don't have to feed the alarm system or pick up their poop."

Sara scowled at the mounds of dog hair she swept up each day from the shepherd/husky mix they had gotten from the shelter. But Larry felt better knowing Sara had company nights he couldn't get home right away. Sara learned to love the mutt and appreciate the added company and security as well. It was a change from her home where no one worried about alarm systems.

Detroit had been fun at first, a great adventure, but as her pregnancy progressed, she found more and more she missed her family and the peace and security of a smaller city. Sometimes she wondered, was this really the right time to have a child? Perhaps they should have waited? Not that they could do anything about it now. The babies were coming regardless, but it hadn't been the plan. She had hoped to have the home more complete, savings in the bank, and maybe be in a position to either quit her job or work part-time. As it was, she had no idea what they were going to do for childcare. At home she would have had her mom to help out. But then her mom was already so busy with Joy's children. And that was another thing. At home their children would have cousins to play with.

"There's plenty of small children in the neighborhood," Larry tried to assuage her concerns. "Our children will have plenty of friends."

"That's not the same as family."

"Sometimes it's better." Sara had to admit that he was right. His mom would gladly move to Detroit, move into their home.

"Just say the word," she had told Larry.

"Mom, you're not moving in with us. What about Dad?"

"He'll fend for himself. It will be good for him, help him appreciate all I do for him. At least let me come for a couple weeks."

"We'll let you know if we need you."

"It's my first grandchildren. Sara's mom already has grandchildren." Yes, there were some advantages to being in Detroit, over an hour drive from the in-laws. Far enough that they can't come over every day, but close enough that they could go home after their visit instead of staying overnight.

"Your mom is ... overwhelming," Sara had said when they had first discussed the possibility of her help.

"Go ahead and say it. Mom can be overbearing," Larry agreed.

"I mean, she rearranged the kitchen when she came to visit and then proceeded to our bedroom."

"I know. It's her way of showing love, helping out. Give it time. You'll learn how to deal with her." Sara doubted that but held her tongue.

But was this the right time to have a baby? And not one, but two? She still had so much to learn, was just beginning to sell her art work. That would be at an end, she figured: it couldn't continue with two babies to take care of.

"You worry too much," Larry told her. Paralysis by analysis, Larry would tease her about her tendency to analyze and plan to the point where she couldn't move. "If we waited for the right time, we may never have children. There never will be a right time, but there's also never a wrong time to have a baby."

"I just want everything to be perfect for these babies."

"It will be. With you as the mother, how could it not be?"

"I'm far from perfect."

"You're closer to it than I am. Besides, no one is perfect. That's just life. You do the best you can in this imperfect world, filled with imperfect people. But our babies will be perfect because they will be ours."

"But," Sara began.

"No buts," Larry said. "These babies will be, already are, loved."

That hushed Sara's fears for a while but she continued to fuss about the nursery, picking the perfect gender neutral colors, scrubbing every corner, keeping the dog out, carefully selecting a crib for the babies to share, curtains and a rocking chair.

"You realize that you won't be able to keep Blaze away from the babies forever," Larry warned as Sara barricaded the dog from the room with a pressure gate. "Besides, children that grow up around pets have stronger immune systems."

"Humor me. I'd like to have one room that isn't full of dog hair. At least for a while."

As her stomach expanded, Sara found it more and more difficult to climb the multiple sets of stairs in their three-level home. "Whose idea was it to put my studio in the top floor," she complained to Blaze as he followed her up and down the stairs. She knew full well whose idea it had been, remembering how Larry had escorted her upstairs and surprised her with the room.

"It's good exercise," Larry insisted. "Just think of all the money we can save by not going to the gym to work out. Enough of a work out climbing our stairs."

Sara didn't laugh at his poor attempt at humor.

"You try carrying an extra twenty pounds around in your stomach and see how funny it is," she complained.

Still she had little to complain about. Larry was thoughtful and attentive, catering to her many whims and cravings. Whenever she caught herself snapping at him, she would go from anger to tears.

"I'm so sorry. I've been a beast. You are so good to me," she would cry. Larry wasn't sure which he disliked more, the irrational anger or weepy tears.

"Just hormones," one of his married colleagues assured him.

"And when it's done you'll have a baby girl or a baby boy. There's nothing like that first time you hold your baby in your arms," Don, his boss, said.

"Yeah, and then there's post-partum depression. You think she's moody now," another said.

"Cut it out. Don't scare him," Don said.

"Yeah, well enjoy it now, because once those babies get here there will be no more sleep, no more going out, no more sex."

"Isn't it time to get back to work." Don sent his employees back to their cubicles. "Don't listen to them. Everything will be fine. Being a dad is the greatest thing that can happen to a man."

Don placed his hand on Larry's shoulder, "You'll be a great dad."

Larry just breathed. If only he could believe that.

Chapter 27

Kathleen came home from her night out to an ambulance in front of her home. The past two months had been filled with work, homework and exams. She had been treating herself to a night out before having to study again. The relaxation from the brief reprieve quickly dissipated at the sound of sirens and flashing lights.

"What is it?" she gasped as she made her way past the flashing red lights and the local fire department personnel that were gathered outside. She arrived inside in time to see her grandpa being carried out on a gurney.

"You family?" one of the firefighters asked her.

"Yes, that's my grandfather." Her mom was throwing a coat on over her pajamas, preparing to ride along.

"Thank God, you're here, Kathleen. I'm riding in the ambulance with Grandpa. Would you bring me a change of clothing and meet us at the hospital? Scott can come with you," Esther said as she followed the paramedics.

"What is it?" Kathleen asked as they rolled the gurney out the door.

"Possible heart attack," Esther said. "We'll know better once we get to the hospital."

Esther was happy to see them when they arrived, especially happy to change out of her pajamas.

"We better call your brother, but tell him not to come. There's nothing he can do here and there's no one to stay with the kids. The morning will be soon enough for him to join us. And call Josh, but tell him to stay at school. There's no need for him to rush home," Esther barked out orders.

Kathleen was surprised at how collected her mother was. It wasn't until Peter arrived that she allowed herself to fall apart, but only for a moment. She hugged Peter, cried, then wiped her tears.

The doctor came out and spoke to them.

"It was his heart. He has suffered a mild heart attack. Fortunately you recognized the symptoms right away and got help. That prevented further damage. We are going to continue to monitor his heart before deciding what to do. He may need a pacemaker and a stent to keep the blood flowing to his heart. We'll know more in the morning. For now, we are moving him to the Cardiac Care Unit. Do you want to see him before we move him?"

They went in.

"You gave us a scare, old man," Esther said.

"I'm too tough to die," Erick commented.

"That's right. You need to stick around for my wedding," Esther reminded him.

"And for when I get married someday," Scott added.

"I'll see what I can do. What about you, Kathleen?"

"If you wait for me to get married, you'll be here forever."

"Sounds like a good idea to me," Esther said.

"Forever might be a bit much to ask," Erick said. "I'll settle for a few more good years."

Kathleen had Peter take her mom and Scott home. She waited for her grandpa to get settled in to CCU then took up her post in the corner.

"You aren't supposed to be here," a nurse informed her. Kathleen stood up.

"I'll sit quiet here in this corner. You won't even know I'm here."

"It's against regulations," the nurse continued, but then she was called out for an emergency. Kathleen slid back into the corner as she said she would.

Seeing the ambulance and her grandfather being carried out had upset her. She realized Grandpa was old, but then he had always been old in her mind, from her earliest memories. She hadn't thought that he might die. He didn't strike her as being any older now than he had been when she was a child. He was the only father she knew. She remembered her conversation with Dale. She didn't know why Grandpa had not been the father to her that he had been to Dale. Maybe because she remembered her dad whereas Dale hadn't. Maybe because she never let him be a father to her. And soon it would be too late.

She fell asleep, crouched into the corner, with her coat as her pillow, resting her head against the wall until woken by her grandfather's nurse.

"You can't sleep here. You have to leave." This time Kathleen didn't fight it. She went into the family waiting room, curled up in a chair and went back to sleep. That was where Peter found her the next morning.

"Your mother's with your grandfather. She sent me in search of you. Pastor Joe's with her. Maybe you should go home and get some sleep."

"How's Gramps?"

"As far as I know, the same as last night. The doctor hasn't been in yet."

"Then I'll wait until the doctor comes."

"Suit yourself," Peter said. "At least let me treat you to breakfast."

"That does sound good," Kathleen agreed. They checked with Esther to see if she wanted to join them.

"No, I'm fine. I had something to eat before I came," she said. "I don't want to take a chance on missing the doctor."

That left Kathleen alone with Peter. She wasn't sure about this. If her stomach hadn't been growling, she probably would have thought better of it and stayed with her mom.

They went to the hospital cafeteria where Kathleen loaded up on scrambled eggs, bacon, toast and coffee.

"Not much of an appetite, I see," Peter joked. Kathleen ignored him.

"Got to keep my energy up," she said.

"You know, Kathleen, we haven't had much time to talk, just the two of us." Peter sat down across from her.

Oh, no, Kathleen thought, here comes the stepdad speech.

"Once your mom and I get married, I'll be your stepdad. You okay with that?"

"Why wouldn't I be? You're not marrying me, you're marrying my mother."

"I'll still be your stepfather."

"What does that mean at my age? It's not like you will be going to my basketball games or taking me fishing."

"Do you want me to take you fishing?"

"No, I hate fishing."

"Okay, so what would you like me to do?"

"Nothing. I'm getting along just fine. I don't need a stepdad."

"Well, then, I hope we can be friends."

"Sure, friends. All that matters is that my mom is happy."

"And that she is."

"That better not change."

"Not if I can help it."

Kathleen finished off her plate. They got a coffee for her mom and joined her upstairs.

Chapter 28

Kathleen looked through the stack of papers. They were finalizing their application for 501c3 status. Peter and Joe were there as chair and vice chair of the board of directors for the proposed non-profit. Esther and Leticia were there, along with Leticia's brother, George, and another lawyer, a friend of his who specialized in non-profit organizations and was helping them through the process.

Kathleen was impatient with the slow pace.

"Actually, in terms of most new non-profits I've been involved with, this is extremely quick," Joe told her at their last meeting when Kathleen had complained. "You take months creating the vision, a mission statement and plan, and gathering local support. Only then do you incorporate and seek a 501c3. You're lucky if you're ready to submit after a year."

"Well, we don't have that kind of time," Kathleen stated. Through her class not only was she learning about non-profit management, she was learning about for-profit businesses that support non-profit.

"But that's not what we want," she stated at the previous board meeting. "We want the non-profit to help keep the building open. If the building were profitable, we wouldn't be having this discussion or all of these meetings." Kathleen was definitely not a meeting person. She preferred making the decisions and going ahead on her own. Peter and Joe repeatedly had to remind her of the need to bring issues and decisions to the board.

"You will never build support if you don't share the decision-making responsibility," Peter constantly told her. "Let us help you." Kathleen wanted help, but only on her terms.

"What we are looking at is something of a hybrid," the non-profit lawyer explained. "If we are to make it in this business climate, we need to be creative, diversify, try different tactics."

"In other words, we can't put all of our eggs in one basket," Peter said.

Kathleen hated Peter's clichés, but she was listening.

"We can't expect a non-profit to be able to support a large building, not right away anyway," he added.

"Right," Joe joined in. "Even United Way struggles to maintain their building, and that's with other non-profit groups renting spaces. That's not the model we want."

"So what do we do?" Kathleen questioned.

"We can go ahead with applying for non-profit status for Joy's Center for Healing and the Arts, but keep the dance studio separate and continue to find renters," Joe said.

"Why are we even bothering with non-profit status then?" Kathleen continued to question.

"So we can apply for grants and fundraise," Joe explained.

"Yes, but if the non-profit isn't going to be profitable ..."

"It's just one piece of a larger pie," Peter clarified. "The non-profit will pay rent for space and will bring more traffic into the building which will then in turn bring in more businesses."

"And it's a way to give back to the community," Leticia added. Kathleen wasn't interested in giving back to the community. What has the community done for me, she thought.

"Joy would have loved it," Esther added. "She would love knowing that children who may not ever have had a chance to learn dance, would now have the opportunity." Esther had Kathleen there. She would do this for Joy. She was doing everything for Joy.

"I know it's a bit muddy right now. It's not exactly clear how it is all going to shake out in the end. That's why we need to make sure there is room within our application to allow for future organizations and to have other non-profits operate under the Center at some point," Joe said. Kathleen shook her head at this, but didn't interrupt.

"We've got room for that, don't we, Steve?" Joe directed his question to the lawyer who was filing the application for them.

"That's right," Steve affirmed what Joe had said.

"So we submit the application and sit on our hands waiting for the IRS to get back to us," Kathleen commented.

"No," Leticia said, "We keep doing what we've been doing and we can start adding in preparation for receiving non-profit status. What about holding a dance camp over spring break? We can offer it for free to children in poor areas?"

Kathleen grimaced at the word free. "How can we afford this?"

"We can if the instructors volunteer their time," Esther said. "It's a great idea. We are usually closed over spring break. All it would take is to open the doors."

"How will we get the kids?" Kathleen asked.

"I'll take care of that," Leticia said. "There are lots of kids in my church and in the neighborhood around the church. We could even use the church bus to bring the kids here. I just have to okay it with my pastor. Or we could bring the dance studio to the church. Hold classes in the community room. That way we wouldn't even have to heat our building."

"It would be a lot of good PR for the dance studio," Esther added. "And would help when we start fundraising." So the papers were filed and the dance camp was born.

Kathleen remembered another meeting over a month ago. A meeting with Delbert, Jerome and their accountant. This trip had been strictly business as Kathleen had driven up during the day.

"So what do you want the books to say?" the accountant had asked her.

"What do you mean?" Kathleen asked.

"I mean, I can make the books say whatever you want. Do you want to be profitable? Do you want to show a loss?"

"Profitable. I want it to appear the dance studio is profitable, even though it isn't," Kathleen said.

"Remember, the dance studio is profitable. It's the building that is losing money," Delbert clarified.

"That's all I need to know." The accountant then proceeded to show Kathleen how to show a profit when there wasn't one, to cook the books, as Peter would say, Kathleen thought to herself.

She was juggling so much at the Center. There was the non-profit process, but there also was the operation of the dance studio, increased classes which meant more pay roll and more expenses along with the additional revenue. The top floor of the building now consisted of the two classrooms and a small office. The gift shop had been moved to the second floor to make more space for the classrooms. But now they needed someone to be in the store and to have hours. Before it had been open when the dance classes were in sessions and either Kathleen or Esther had taken care of sales. When someone wanted to buy something, they had got them from the office. But with the additional classes and having the gift shop on the second floor, Esther and Kathleen were running up and down the stairs and weren't as available to handle sales.

They had started with volunteers from among members of the Breast Cancer Support Group and the parents who hung out in the studio while their children were taking classes. As the business was growing, they were going to need to hire someone soon. They also had an art gallery on the second floor where Sara's art work was on sale. They had art work by other local artists available as well, but once again, they couldn't just leave the room open now that it had been moved from the third floor, so that required volunteers as well and would eventually mean more staff.

They had a ceramic store on the first floor along with the pottery store. Both used the separate classrooms Kathleen had created in the basement so the store owners had the option of offering classes to the public. Kathleen was talking with a naturopath and a massage therapist about moving their businesses into the center. If these came through they would be closer to full and well on their way to profitability, as long as the boiler continued to chug along.

Given this, Kathleen was doubly unsure about setting up a non-profit. Leticia was the force behind this.

"Wouldn't it be great if we could have a performance space in the Center," Ava suggested. There was the ballroom/banquet space on the second floor, with high ceilings and chandeliers.

"We could have a stage on one side with moveable chairs, keeping the room flexible for rentals. It could be rented for weddings or other receptions, but also used for recitals and performances by small theater groups," Ava continued.

"We already have the kitchen from the restaurant. It would be too much to set it up as a commercial kitchen, but it could be a serving kitchen where we could bring in food from caterers for rentals," Esther added.

Kathleen liked the idea despite who had suggested it. "But it would require money to fix it up."

"We might be able to get grant money to do this," Ava suggested.

"Once we get our 501c3," Leticia added.

Kathleen approved the paperwork.

Chapter 29

Scott missed hanging out with Stephanie, but he told himself it was for the best. He had other friends. They all supported him in his resolve.

"She's no good for you," his friend Roger told him. Josh had been thankful to find this out over Christmas.

"She's self-destructive," Josh told him. "You can't stop her and you might get hurt if you are in her path."

"How are things with you and Stephanie?" his Uncle Dale had asked him.

"She has her own friends," Scott stated. Dale didn't pursue it. "I guess it wasn't meant to be," Scott added.

Scott watched Stephanie all the while. When he did see her, she was hanging out with a whole new group of friends. Somehow she had made her way into the "in" crowd. Scott didn't know how she had managed that. She was hanging out with seniors, partying hard. He didn't fit in with that group.

There was talk of some seniors going to Florida for spring break. Joe had squashed that idea.

"No way, you are way too young to be going away for 'spring break'."

"Dad, Shanna's parents will be there the whole time."

"And just who is this Shanna? Have I met her? And what about her parents?"

"You're such a Nazi, Dad. I can't go anywhere or do anything."

"If that's the case, you might as well be grounded since you don't go anywhere or do anything." Joe started to send her to her room, then thought better of it.

"Wait. You aren't escaping that easily. You're going to stay down here in the living room and watch TV with me and your sister."

Stephanie plopped down on the couch and sat with her hands crossed in front of her all night until allowed to go to her room.

"Can I go now?"

"Sure, it's time for bed." It had not been a pleasant night, but at least this way he was able to keep an eye on her, which he couldn't do when she was barricaded in her room. He had caught her sneaking out too many times to feel comfortable with her alone in her room all night.

Stephanie still had her ways, sneaking out when her dad had meetings at church. Michelle was sworn to secrecy.

Her revenge on her dad for not letting her go south for spring break was to find every way within her means to annoy him when he was home, and to sneak out to every party she could find during the week. It was Pastor Joe's busiest week of the year, Holy Week, and Stephanie knew it. He struggled to complete all of the necessary preparations for the additional services while keeping an eye on his willful daughter.

"Maybe I should have let her go," he told himself one night after yet another altercation with Stephanie. "I would have to deal with the repercussions when she came home, but at least I would have had a peaceful Holy Week." But then he dismissed the thought. "Better to have her here causing trouble than to worry about what trouble she might be in. Time enough for that when she goes away to college."

Joe came home from the Good Friday Service exhausted. There had been the Maundy Thursday service the night before and another service scheduled for this night. At least at that one he didn't have to preach. It consisted of hymns around the cross. All he had to do was show up. He could have ordered his daughters to attend, but it was bad enough having a snarling teen at home. He didn't need one at church, too.

He had no energy to deal with his daughter, needed to rest in preparation for Easter Sunday. Stephanie was counting on that. She quietly sat through dinner with her family and cleared the table and loaded the dishwasher without voicing a complaint. Joe figured she was up to something but didn't have the strength to deal with it. When she said she was going to her room to read, he didn't even challenge her.

Once he left for the seven o'clock service, Stephanie was down the stairs and out the door.

"Where are you going?" Michelle asked.

"Church."

"Sure, dressed like that." Stephanie had on her shortest skirt and a top that hugged her chest like another layer of skin.

"We both know this is Dad's busiest time of the year, so neither of us are going to bother him, especially you," Stephanie threatened.

"Enjoy church," Michelle said as she curled up on the couch with a book.

Her dad came home about nine and found Michelle still reading on the couch.

"Good book?" he asked.

"Yep," Michelle said without looking up.

"No babysitting job tonight?"

"Not tonight."

"It's unusual to have you home on a Friday night."

"My regulars are gone for spring break."

"Oh, yeah. Heard anything out of Stephanie?"

"Not a peep."

"That's good," Joe proceeded to his room to change his clothes. He wasn't surprised when he got no answer to his knock on Stephanie's door.

"Stephanie, I'm making popcorn. Come on down and join us." He wasn't surprised when he opened her door and saw she was gone. Nothing surprised him where Stephanie was concerned. He had suspected as much. What was he to do?

Tomorrow would be another day to fight. It would be soon enough. For tonight he was going to relax and try not to worry about his wayward daughter. He waited up, expecting another call from law enforcement officials.

When would be his Easter, he wondered? Where was his resurrection?

Chapter 30

"So much for pinky swears," Dale said as he ran into Kathleen on his way to the ballroom dance class.

"Mom's stronger than a pinky swear," Kathleen said.

"She has more power in a single look than I have in my right arm."

"Yeah, my arm still hurts from her twisting it behind my back." They were still joking as they entered the classroom, feigning injury as they approached Esther and Peter.

"You better not ever cross my mom," Dale told Peter as he massaged his arm.

"Ha, ha," Esther responded. "Remember, I brought you into this world. I can take you out."

"So nice of you two to accommodate your mother's wishes," Peter said.

"Accommodate? More like being black-mailed," Kathleen said.

"Enough already. I'm glad you're here," Esther said. "Now hush, class is starting."

Kathleen and Dale paired up as the class began. As they danced, Esther and Peter looked over at Joe and Ava then back at Dale and Kathleen.

"It's just not right for brothers and sisters to dance together," Esther said.

"My thoughts as well," Peter agreed. They danced over to Dale and Kathleen and broke in.

"Dale, I want to practice dancing with you," Esther said as she took him away. Peter danced with Kathleen. Then both couples moved towards Joe and Ava.

"Pastor," Esther said. "I need to discuss some details about the wedding."

"Right now?" Joe asked.

"Yes, now," she said, taking him by the hand and leaving Dale with Ava. "Now don't they look good together?" Esther nodded at the pair.

"So, this was a ruse to get Dale and Ava together," Joe said.

"Who said it was about Dale and Ava," Esther said as she switched partners again, leaving Joe with Kathleen.

"Now that's better," Esther said to Peter as they observed the newly formed couples.

"You can lead a horse to water ..." Peter started.

"I know, you can't make them drink, but if they don't ever go to the water to start with ...? Sometimes love needs help."

"We'll see."

Dale had been avoiding Ava since that coffee date. He felt guilty about not calling her, when he thought about it. For the most part, he avoided thinking about it by burying himself in work. What time he had outside of work was committed to family.

He hadn't been able to avoid all mention of Ava at home as Jacob talked about the recital and how Ava was helping with it. Even Ashley seemed to be coming around where Ava was concerned, admitting that she wasn't so bad.

"I'm sorry I haven't called," he said awkwardly as he tried to avoid stepping on her feet.

"That's okay. There was no commitment. I didn't expect a call."

"You didn't?"

"No, I understand why you didn't call."

"Do you really?"

"I understand it's a lot to ask of someone."

"I've been really busy."

"You don't have to explain yourself to me."

The fact that she was being so understanding made him feel even worse rather than better. Maybe he had been wrong, he told himself.

"I think we've been outmaneuvered," Kathleen said to Joe.

"You think so?" Joe smiled.

"They do look good together, Dale and Ava." Dale tripped over his own feet as he struggled to dance. Kathleen laughed. "Well, Ava looks good."

"What about us? I think the plot extends beyond Dale and Ava."

"You think so?" Kathleen shook her head. "My mother never gives up."

"She is pretty persistent."

"Some call it stubborn."

"That too," Joe agreed. "What's Scott up to?"

"Keeping his grandpop company, playing cards."

"How is Erick?"

"As ornery as ever. What about Stephanie?"

"You don't want to go there."

"Try me."

"I don't want to go there." Joe avoided bumping into Dale and Ava. "There must be something more pleasant to talk about, anything. How about the hurricane that hit Fiji?"

"That bad?"

"That bad." They danced in silence. If they didn't talk about their kids, what was left?

They were grateful for the break, joining the other couples.

"Guess it's time for me to rescue my partner," Joe said as he approached Dale and Ava. "That is if you want rescuing?"

"That's all right," Ava said. "I think I'll go home. I've got a splitting headache."

"Okay. I'll get our coats," Joe said as they left.

"What was that about? I thought you liked Dale." Joe asked when they got in his car.

"I've got a headache."

"Really?"

"Really." They drove a while in silence before Joe spoke up.

"What is this really about?"

"Dale's not interested in me."

"He seemed pretty interested from what I saw."

"No, he was just being polite. I told him about my history months ago. He hasn't called me since. I don't blame him. I wouldn't want to date me either, if I were him."

"There's something you aren't telling me." Joe pulled up in front of her apartment building and waited.

"Even if Dale were interested in me, I'm not interested in him."

"That didn't seem to be the case to me."

"Well, it is. He had the perfect wife, whereas I'm ... I'm far from perfect. I wouldn't want to live in her shadow."

"What shadow are you living in?"

"What are you talking about?"

"You tell me. You're hiding something."

"All right. I'll tell you." Joe waited while Ava reached for the words. "I haven't told you everything. When I was in college, I had an abortion." Her calm words sounded strange to her ears. It was as if someone else were talking.

Joe took her hands as she said this.

"I was engaged at the time. My fiancé didn't want the child and talked me into getting the abortion. Then he left me. And now I can't have any children of my own. It's God's punishment."

"I don't believe God works that way."

"Well, it seems that way to me. I deserve to be punished. I don't deserve children."

"Do you also deserve to live your life alone?"

"Yes, I don't deserve love."

"That's your own punishment. You're your own judge and jury, condemning yourself without a hearing. When will you stop punishing yourself?"

"What good would a hearing do? I know what I did. I will live with that guilt for the rest of my life."

"But there is also forgiveness."

"Not for me."

"It's not God who won't forgive you, but yourself. Don't you think you've suffered enough over this?"

"No." Ava continued to stare straight ahead into the darkness.

"Then what will it take for you to finally forgive yourself?"

"I don't know. Some things are unforgiveable."

"Not in God's eyes."

"But in my eyes. It's just how I feel. You can't change my feelings."

"Maybe I can't, but God can."

"Even God can't change this." Ava opened the car door as Joe put his hand on hers again.

"Forgiveness is a slow process. It doesn't happen overnight. Healing is a slow process. It's a slow waltz. Sometimes you go backwards, sometimes sideways before you go forward again. It can't be rushed. But it can help if you have others by your side," he said as he let go of her hand. "I'll pray for you."

Ava hurried out the door without a response, as the tears that had been frozen inside her started to slide down her cheeks.

At the dance class, Peter paired with Kathleen and Esther with Dale.

"This way it won't be the blind leading the blind," Peter said. "I can teach you a few tricks," he told Kathleen.

"I bet you can," Kathleen smiled.

"You appear to be enjoying yourself."

"Maybe I'm just grateful that Grandpop's okay."

"Doesn't have anything to do with that pastor?"

"Of course not," Kathleen insisted. "First Jacob, then Grandpop. My mom says bad things happen in threes," Kathleen changed the subject. "Wonder what the third might be," she added.

"Bite your tongue. We are done with bad news for a while. Your family has had more than their share. No more hospital visits, no more rides in ambulances, no deaths or close encounters with death."

"It has been a rough few years. You sure you want to be part of this mess we call family."

"Every family has its messes to deal with. You just don't see them unless you are in the thick of it. Life is so much more interesting with a few messes here and there."

Just then the boiler made a strange gurgling sound and a loud pop and stopped running.

"What was that?" Kathleen said, afraid she knew what it was. "Don't tell me the boiler just died. Number three."

"That's a silly superstition," Peter insisted.

"Then what was that?"

"So how are things with you and Ava?" Esther asked Dale.

"If you must know, she had cancer a few years ago. She's cancer-free now but who knows how long that will be? I can't go through that again." Dale decided to get right to it, knowing his mother would be relentless in her questions.

"So are you going to rule out every woman who has had a past cancer diagnosis? What else are you going to rule out? Anyone who's been in a car accident? Or been sick at any time in their life? You know there's no guarantee that you won't walk out of this building and be hit by a car. Look at what happened to Pastor Joe's wife? There's no guarantee that you won't have a heart attack like Grandpop."

"Grandpop is old."

"Bad example. But there are no guarantees in this life. There's no guarantee that Ava will remain cancer-free, but there's no guarantee she won't, just as there's no guarantee that you won't get cancer at some point in your life."

"You aren't going to let go of this, are you, Mom?"

"Let me continue. I can guarantee that if you continue to hide from life in that business of yours, you will die sad and alone, and that includes your children. Do you think I don't see how Ashley looks when you work late every night? They'll grow up before you know it, and you'll have missed it. Life is full of hurt. If you love, you will hurt, but it's worth the price."

Just then they heard the same gurgle and pop that Kathleen and Peter had heard.

"What was that?" Esther asked.

Chapter 31

Dale, Kathleen, Esther and Peter left the dance class and went to the basement to check the boiler. Fortunately they were past the coldest part of the year and still had electricity, so the dance class had been able to continue without heat.

"Looks like it's gone," Dale said after his inspection.

"I know. The last time I had it repaired, the repairman said he doubted he would be able to fix it again," Kathleen said.

"When was that?" Peter asked.

"Back in December. That was why I needed the loan. That and for some other repairs."

"Why didn't you tell me that then?"

"I didn't want anyone to know about all the extra expenses. I didn't want them worrying."

"But wouldn't that be in the financial reports? I don't remember seeing any record of boiler repairs?"

"No, I kept my own accounting of them. Even Mom didn't know about it."

"Why didn't you ask me to look at the boiler?" Dale asked.

"You already put so much of your own money into this building. Besides, I knew how painful it was for you to come inside."

"I couldn't avoid it forever. Sometimes you just have to get through the pain," Dale replied, not looking at Esther.

"You've been carrying the weight for this building by yourself for far too long," Peter said. "Let us help. That's what you have a board for."

"Well, I guess maybe now is the time for that second mortgage you talked about before, Mom," Kathleen said.

"Can't," Esther said.

"Why not? You offered several times."

"Because I already took out a second mortgage," Esther explained.

"What? When did you do that?" Kathleen asked.

"February," Esther stated.

"After we had talked about it?" Peter asked.

"Yes," Esther admitted.

"And we agreed that it was a bad idea," Peter said.

"You agreed. I didn't agree to anything."

"Where is the money, Mom?" Kathleen asked.

"I've been adding it, a couple thousand a month. I made it look like we were taking in more each month than we were from the additional classes. I thought that then you would finally agree to take a salary."

"You did what?" Kathleen said, then burst out laughing. "Mom, you've been cooking the books. I'd be crying if it wasn't so absurd. I can't believe you did that."

"It's really not that hard if you know what you are doing. Any good accountant can do it." At this Esther started laughing along with Kathleen.

"I don't know what you two are laughing about," Peter stated. "You've both committed a crime."

"So arrest us. Who's going to report us? You?" Esther said.

"No, but we better get the books straight. First thing tomorrow, I want to look at them. We need to know just how bad this is. Then we need to hold an emergency board meeting to decide what to do." Peter turned to Dale. "Dale, can you get us some numbers on a boiler?"

"I'll see what I can do," Dale said. Meanwhile, Esther and Kathleen were still fighting laughter.

"I don't see what's so funny. Do you understand how serious this is?" Peter asked them.

"No, but I'm sure I'll hear about it until I do," Esther responded. "I just can't help it. It's just the stress of the past few years, I guess. Like daughter, like mother," Esther stated and stifled a laugh.

Things didn't look so funny in the morning as they gathered in the cold building to go over the finances. Still, Kathleen felt a strange calm through it all. Peter, on the other hand, was far from confident. It was as if she had shifted the concerns in regards to the Center to him. It felt good to rely on someone else for a change.

Peter was not happy when Esther and Kathleen came forward with their separate accounts.

"Can the two of you come up with an accurate accounting for the past six months? No cooked books. I want them combined into one. Show the loans, how much was spent on repairs, how much actual income the Dance Studio had. It's a good thing we haven't been audited," he mumbled to himself after dispensing orders to Esther and Kathleen. "We have to figure out how to explain this to the board."

"Isn't it better that they don't know?" Esther suggested. "The fewer people in on this, the better. Let's keep it in the family."

"You forget, once we get non-profit status, this will no longer be a 'family' business. As a non-profit our books need to be open to review. Even as a family business there is accountability," Peter explained.

"That's why we have you, dear, to keep us on the straight and narrow," Esther said. The giddiness from the previous night was gone and the seriousness of the situation was setting in, but she wasn't worried yet.

"I think we need to let the executive committee in on this," Peter said. "The rest of the board doesn't need to know the details, especially about the falsified books, but they should know." Peter contacted Joe, the vice-chair, and Ava, the secretary-treasurer and set a meeting for that afternoon. "Hopefully by then we'll have a better idea where we stand financially, and maybe Dale will have some leads on a boiler."

Esther and Kathleen worked all morning combining books to get an accurate picture of the Center's finances.

"It's not as bad as it sounded last night," Esther explained to Peter before the meeting. "We've been very careful with expenses. We've got the $5,000 loan you co-signed with Kathleen and I've only used around $6,000 out of the money from the second mortgage. That's a deficit of $11,000. I still have $14,000 left on the $20,000 I took out that can be used for the new boiler."

"Yes, but we have all of the back pay we owe Kathleen. By the way, that will not continue. As chair of the board, I insist that Kathleen start getting paid and we have an accounting of all we owe her."

"But we don't have the money," Kathleen insisted.

"Let me worry about that."

Peter explained to Joe and Ava about the situation.

"I don't think I need to tell you that this is to go no further than this room."

Dale had spent the morning looking for boilers. He joined them that afternoon despite Ashley's protests.

"But Dad, you promised."

"I know, but this is an emergency."

"There's always something," Ashley pouted and complained when left once again with their babysitter, Michelle.

"I know. My dad's the same. They mean well though," Michelle said.

Dale was all too aware of Ashley's displeasure, especially after what his mom had said last night. He promised himself he would make it up to her. How, he wasn't sure, but he was determined to keep this promise.

"What did you find out?" Peter asked Dale.

"I can get one for around $30,000. That's with my company providing free labor. Hopefully there will be no other problems when we install it. You never know what you are going to run into when you put a piece of new equipment into an old building."

"We can't ask that of you," Kathleen said.

"You aren't asking, I'm offering. I have an investment in the Center. My children are attending classes here. It's their mother's legacy that we are talking about." Ava looked aside as he said that.

"Okay, that's not too bad. But what are we going to do in the meantime till we get the money for the boiler. I know it's not winter, but we still need heat," Esther said. They were all wearing coats.

"I can finance the boiler for now. That way we can get it installed on Monday as soon as it gets here so we won't have to cancel any classes," Dale said.

"Again, we can't ..." Kathleen started.

"You'll owe me."

"But what if we can't make it, if the center closes?"

"Then you'll pay me back with the proceeds from the sale of the building," Dale said.

"It's a risk," Kathleen said.

"One I'm willing to take."

"Okay, it sounds like that is settled, but what do we do about this deficit? How do we raise the money to pay it back?" Peter asked.

"Wait," Joe interrupted. "If we have the boiler repaired on Monday, there will be less incentive to contribute to buy a new one."

"So you're saying?" Peter said.

"I'm saying, uncomfortable people will be more likely to dip into their pockets. It's not so cold that we have to worry about frozen pipes. A little cold won't hurt and may be a good motivator for people to donate."

"I always knew there was a reason we had to sit in a hot stuffy church when the air conditioning failed last summer," Esther said.

"Good stewardship of church resources," Joe grinned. "It just makes sense. Besides it is too much of a risk for Dale."

"Okay, so we won't get a new boiler right away," Peter said.

"And the other thing is, if we are going to fundraise, why not figure out all the repairs that are needed and put it into a capital campaign."

"Did you learn that in seminary?" Peter asked.

"No, but it's common practice. Rather than coming back for something every few months, you lay out a campaign. It shows you are planning for the future – not just patching holes."

"What do we include in this capital campaign?" Esther asked.

"What do we need to bring the whole building up to the state we want it in, to make it attractive to renters?"

"Well, the ballroom requires a lot of work, but once completed we could make money by renting it out," Ava suggested.

"We could also use it for our recitals and save money on renting a space," Esther added.

"Ava, can you come up with some figures for how much that would cost?" Peter asked.

"I'll look into it," she said.

"We've already painted everything. I think the wiring is good. The boiler was the big ticket item. Then, maybe some plumbing," Kathleen began.

"I can take care of that," Dale offered.

"The next big thing is the elevator. I don't know how long it will be functional," Kathleen continued. "And it's small for wheel chairs. They barely fit. And insulation and new windows would be great and help cut down on heating costs. And the parking lot ..."

"Okay, I got it. There's a lot of work to be done," Peter stopped her.

"We could have three phases to our campaign. The first will be the boiler and the ball room. Phase II will be handicap accessibility. That's a must for federal funding if we go that way. Phase III can be insulation, windows and the parking lot," Joe proposed.

"Let's put it all together and call an emergency board meeting on Monday," Peter suggested.

Chapter 32

On Monday it was actually warmer outside than it was inside the drafty old building. Kathleen had the instructors open the windows to bring in the warmer air until it turned colder. The students danced with jackets on, but overall it wasn't too bad.

When the board members entered the cold building, they knew something was up even before Peter began to talk.

"We have some problems. Our boiler gave out over the weekend. Even with donated labor, it will cost over $30,000, which, of course, we don't have. The other problem is that a review of the books found some accounting errors. These errors have been corrected but it seems we've been operating at a deficit of over $10,000. That deficit has been taken care of by loans, but we can't continue this way. We need to pay back the loans. And last, as you know, our Executive Director has graciously been serving with no pay. I know this is common with non-profit start-ups, but it has to stop."

"What are we going to do?" one board member asked.

"But we've got so many programs just getting off the ground," another said.

"That's why I called this meeting. The executive committee met over the weekend and we've come up with a proposal for a capital campaign." Peter turned the meeting over to Joe to explain the plan. After Joe finished, Peter took the floor back.

"In regards to the deficit and the salary for our Executive Director, income will increase once the necessary repairs are done. Renting the ball room will be a source of income. We won't be able to pay off the loans right away, but we will pay a small portion on them each month. We also propose including a twenty hours a week position for our Executive Director. As the center raises more funds the position will be increased to full time."

"In order to meet our goals we will need to do some fundraising," he added.

"But we don't have our 501c3 yet?"

"We'll just have to let people know their donation isn't tax deductible yet," Peter explained.

"When will we get it?"

"Anybody's guess. It's the IRS after all. They take their time unless they are taking your money and charging interest."

"If I might have a word," Pastor Elwood stood up to address the board. "On behalf of the children of my church and the neighborhood, I want to thank you for the dance camp last week. It was well attended and greatly appreciated," Pastor Elwood began. Peter knew better than to interrupt Pastor Elwood when he was making a speech. He waited while the pastor took his time, elaborating on how much his congregation appreciated the dance camp. Slowly he made his way to his point. "I want you to know that Congressman Conroy's parents are members of my church congregation. I'm sure they could get him to intervene on our behalf and speed up the process for our 501c3 application."

"That would be great. It's certainly worth a try," Peter said. "Thank you, Pastor."

Pastor Elwood sat down amid thankyous.

"What if we had a dinner and a silent auction?" Ava suggested. "We could do it in the ballroom in May, borrow tables and chairs from the church, tell everyone about our vision for the Center. It could be a great kick-off event. I could probably arrange for entertainment too."

"Another good idea," Peter said.

The rest of the meeting was spent planning for the silent auction and other fundraisers.

Chapter 33

At seven months Sara looked and felt like a beached whale when her midwife confined her to bed rest.

"We want to give those babies as much time to develop as possible. You don't want to do anything that would cause an early labor."

Aware of the possibility, Sara had already made arrangements to work part-time from home. Larry could pick up any assignments that couldn't be sent electronically. She set up a temporary studio/office in their living room. Each morning she would slide down the stairs on her rear then stay on the first floor until time to crawl back up for bed. She spent most of her day on the couch, sketch book on her lap.

It was as if the knowledge set off a creative spark within her as she found herself sketching again, this time sketches of mothers, fat with child, and twins, playing together in the womb, fighting, romping in a watery bath.

"I'm giving these to Kathleen for the silent auction they are holding for Joy's Center," she told Larry. She hated the fact that she couldn't do more, but what she could do, she did. She also recruited donations from her artist friends. "It's to support a center for the arts," she told them.

Perhaps the hardest part of bed rest was not being able to go home for the weekends. She missed her family, missed her hometown.

"Enjoy it while you can. Once those babies are born there will be no rest," her mom had told her. She remembered Joy saying pretty much the same thing in the past about her babies.

"If you need help, my mom would be happy to stay," Larry had suggested when Sara complained about not being able to get everything done that she felt needed to get done.

"No way." She wanted help but the help she wanted was from her own mother who was busy with Joy's children.

She had been happy when her parents had come for Easter weekend.

"Don't you worry about anything. We'll take care of meals. And if there's anything we can do to help get ready for those babies, let us know," her mom had said. Larry's parents had also come for Easter dinner. Clara had been in touch with Sara's mom and together they had planned the meal. Sara hadn't been sure about the extra people in the house. Her parents were company. Larry's made it a crowd, but she was a good sport about it and enjoyed being pampered by two moms.

"What a luxury," she had said as she sat down to Easter dinner.

"Don't get used to it," Larry cautioned with a smile.

"What do you mean, don't get used to it," his mother said. "Once those babies are born, you could have help full time, around the clock."

"Mom, I already told you we would think about it," Larry told her.

"You better think about it too, Clara. You're not as young as you used to be," Larry's dad said to his wife. "It's been a long time since you've taken care of a baby. You forget how hard it is, right Mary?" He addressed Sara's mom.

"It has been too long since I've held a baby in my arms," Clara said.

"Yes, it is harder when you are older. There's a reason why you have children while you are young," Mary said. She never said anything around Dale, but it was a challenge watching Grace as much as she did, even with Esther's help. "But it's also a blessing."

"I can't wait to hold a baby again," Clara said.

"With two of them, there should be ample opportunity," Tom said.

As Larry's parents left, Clara hugged Sara and said, "By the way, I made a few changes to the nursery. You're going to love them."

The babies weren't due till the first of June, but the likelihood was that they would be born earlier than that as the babies outgrew the room in Sara's uterus. Once the ultrasound showed that the babies were big enough to survive on their own, her midwife took her off of bed rest. Sara found it hard to do much more than she had been doing as she waddled from room to room. The stairs were next to impossible to negotiate with the extra weight throwing her off-balance, so she continued to keep her trips up and down to a minimum.

She mistakenly thought that the minute she was off of bed-rest the babies would be born. Instead, after a few days there was no sign of labor except a few Braxton-Hicks pains.

"It's time you get out of here," Larry told her. She hadn't returned to work since she expected the babies to be born any day. "What if we go to your parents' this weekend?"

"Are you sure it's safe?"

"The midwife said you could resume normal activity, so why not? A short trip will do you good."

"I could go to the fundraiser for Joy's Center," Sara said as she kissed Larry.

Chapter 34

Ava was in charge of the entertainment for the dinner/fundraiser. She managed to throw together a makeshift stage along with some lights and a borrowed sound system. She also produced a power point slide-show with pictures of the building as it is now and drawings of what they hoped it would become "with your help."

There were some dance numbers including traditional ballet, Irish dances and modern dance. Patrick brought some of his more experienced dancers to perform and Jerome put together a jazz band for the occasion. Leticia arranged for a group of students from the spring dance camp to come and perform a routine including what she was learning at her dance workshops.

Ava was going to talk about the vision for the new Center, the changes they had already made, the ones they hoped to make.

"Young people who never would have had a chance to take a dance class or play an instrument or have art lessons, all would have the opportunity to do so here. There also will be art therapy and music therapy provided for cancer survivors to enhance their recovery. All we need to make this dream a reality is your support."

"You sound like a natural," Joe told her as she practiced her spiel. "Next time I have a church fundraiser, remind me to call on you."

Dale and Howard helped with the construction of the stage and other odd jobs. Outside of passing acknowledgements when they saw each other at the center, Dale hadn't spoken to Ava since the dance class. He was trying to spend more time at home with his kids, while helping his mother and sister at the center. He started bringing the kids with him when he was there, much as Joy used to. Grace loved the opportunity to run around the large classrooms. Jacob enjoyed being around the other workers, and Ashley was happy to be doing something with her dad.

"It's like it used to be," Jacob said.

"No, it's not, stupid. Mom's not here," Ashley retorted.

"Stop calling me stupid," Jacob cried.

"Sounds pretty much like it used to be," Dale said, as he chastised Ashley. He disagreed with Ashley. Being in this building, in Joy's dance studio, he felt her presence. It accentuated all he had lost and would never have again.

"Ashley, watch Grace for me, will you?" Dale asked, sending Ashley on her way.

"It looks good," Dale told Ava as the finishing touches were put on the room, including table cloths for the borrowed tables and decorations to bring the room to life.

"Just think how much better it will look with a real stage, new tables and chairs and a refinished dance floor," she told him.

"You don't have to convince me," Dale said with a smile. "I meant what I said before. I'm sorry about not calling. I've just been so busy with work and the kids and all."

"I've been busy, too." Ava started to move past him. Dale put his hand on her arm.

"Do you think, maybe, we could try again?"

Ava turned to face him. "I don't know. I'm not sure I want to live in the shadow of your former wife."

"Joy was someone special."

"Her spirit is throughout this building, in all the students whose lives she has touched. Even I can feel it." She turned away from him. "How can I live up to that?"

"No one is asking you to."

"Maybe I'm asking myself." Ava refused to look at him. "Besides there are other things you don't know about me."

"I'd like to find out."

"No, it won't work." This time it was Ava's turn to dismiss Dale. She had already said more than she had intended.

Chapter 35

The evening was a success. Dale hadn't known that Sara was coming until she was wheeled off the elevator. Mary had arranged for the wheel chair.

"Mom, I'm not an invalid," Sara had protested at first.

"Yes, but you can't be climbing all of those stairs at the center. We'll roll you in then once you are in the room, you can do whatever you want."

When Dale saw Sara in a wheel chair, he thought for a moment that it was Joy as he remembered her at Sara's wedding. He shook his head and brushed away a tear as he approached.

"It's so good to see you," he told Sara. "I didn't know you were coming."

"Well, I didn't know either until earlier this week."

"You look great," Dale gave her a kiss on the cheek.

"Seems like it's been forever," Sara commented.

"Far too long. The kids have missed their Aunt Sara."

Ashley and Jacob came running up behind Dale with Grace in tow.

"Aunt Sara, where have you been?" Ashley asked as Larry helped Sara to her feet.

"Aunt Sara's fat," Jacob said to no one in particular when he saw her full frame.

"Jacob, that's rude," Dale chided.

"He's only speaking the truth," Sara laughed. "I'm huge."

"Why?" Jacob asked.

"Because I've got two babies inside me, your cousins."

"Can I see them?" he asked.

"No, stupid. They're still inside her," Ashley scolded.

"You'll see them soon enough," Sara told him.

Mary insisted on bringing the wheel chair into the hall.

"Just in case," she said.

Sara was warmly welcomed by family and friends and was pleased to see people bidding on her sketches. It was also nice to be introduced as an artist, not just Joy's sister. The oil painting she had made for Joy when Joy had been pregnant with Grace had been moved to a prominent position on the wall in the ball room.

As Sara stood in front of the picture, holding onto Larry's arm with one hand, the other wrapped under her belly, it seemed for a moment that it was just her and Joy in the room, Joy pregnant with Grace, Sara pregnant with her twins. Joy smiled at Sara as she reached out to touch the canvas. Tears streamed down her face.

"Are you okay? Maybe this wasn't such a good idea," Larry said.

"No, it was a great idea. It is so good to be here with family," Sara assured him. Larry helped her to her seat with her parents and Dale's family. Kathleen and Esther came over and hugged her.

"So when are the newest additions to the family coming?" Kathleen asked.

"You know, you are still part of the family," Esther added. "You are coming to my wedding, aren't you?"

"The babies could come any time, and I wouldn't miss your wedding," Sara responded. Being back in this building with family brought back so many memories.

Kathleen and Esther spent the evening moving among the tables, talking to guests, answering questions about the center. Joe, Josh, Scott, Stephanie and Michelle were busy waiting tables, bringing drinks, serving food and removing empty plates. Joe was keeping close wraps on Stephanie. Helping out at the fundraiser and church activities was the "community service" he had assigned her after her last altercation with the police. Peter kept Erick and Howard company at their table. When the meal ended and the entertainment began, Esther joined them. Joe, eating with the rest of the wait staff, sought out Kathleen with his eyes and found her sitting with Jerome and the band as they ate, having finished their set of music. Leticia was busy helping Ava with the entertainment. When the Irish dancers were done, Kathleen moved to Patrick's table for the remainder of the entertainment, until called forth by Ava to help with the financial appeal.

Board members were introduced and instructed to pick up the donation envelopes that were on each table once they were filled. There was one last call for bids on silent auction items before closing the bidding.

Sara picked at her food, not really hungry as the babies pushed against her stomach, causing indigestion. As the evening came to a close, she stood up to leave, only to be embarrassed by a spurt of water from between her legs.

"Larry," she whispered, "I think my water just broke." She was then hit with a wave of nausea and cramps. She grasped his arm. "It's good I didn't eat my dinner." She tried to smile.

"Let me get the wheelchair," Larry said, sitting Sara back down.

"What's happening?" Mary asked. "Do we need to call an ambulance?"

"No, she's fine. We can drive her," Larry insisted.

They made their way through the departing crowd, Sara a mixture of apprehension and excitement.

"But what about the midwife?" Sara asked.

"I don't think we can take the chance of driving back to Detroit yet tonight. Let's get you checked out at the hospital here," Larry said.

"But all of our stuff for the babies, it's in Detroit."

"A minor problem. Just breathe."

They had come to the fundraiser with Sara's parents, Tom and Mary. Larry climbed into the back seat with Sara, holding her hand, while Tom drove them to the hospital.

"Can't you go any faster, Dad?" Sara asked.

"Don't you worry, little Sara. The first baby usually takes their time arriving. We have plenty of time to get there." Tom reassured her. Sara was comforted by her dad's words until the next pain hit.

"What's wrong with Aunt Sara?" Jacob asked.

"She's about to have her babies," Dale explained. "She'll be okay."

"Good, then I can play with them," Jacob said.

"Not right away. Remember how Grace was when she was born?"

"I hope she has boys," Jacob added. "There's too many girls in this family."

Dale was helping Ava clean up while Kathleen, Esther and Peter were going over the receipts from the auction and other donations.

"Is there anything else I can do?" he asked as they cleared the last table.

"We do need to take that picture back upstairs, if you don't mind," Ava told him.

"Sure thing," he told her. "You kids stay down here." They were happily playing with Michelle while Joe, Josh, Scott and Stephanie finished in the kitchen. As he carried the picture up the stairs, the burden grew heavier. He remembered all those times, carrying Joy up and down the stairs at home until she was too weak to even do that.

He hung the picture on its spot on the wall, then stood back and looked at it.

His Joy, with rounded belly, in her ballet clothes, dancing on a wire suspended in the air, surrounded by angels. He doubted Sara knew how prophetic her painting would be. They had such hope back then. They were going to beat this cancer, and Joy had for a while, but only for a while.

He remembered the promise he had made with no intention of keeping it.

"I want you to marry again," Joy had told him.

He had agreed just to placate her, but here it was, almost two years since she had died. He wanted to love again, wanted to laugh again and not be buried in sadness, but did he dare?

"There will never be anyone like you," he told the picture.

"I know – but you can, and must, love again," Joy told him.

"It hurts too much."

"That's the price we pay for love. Everything has a price tag."

"Some prices are too high to pay," he told her. For just a moment he thought he smelt the distinctive aroma of cocoa butter, Joy's favorite body lotion. Then it was gone.

"Did you say something?" Ava appeared at the top of the stairs.

"No, nothing."

"We were beginning to worry, you were gone so long." She looked back and forth between him and the picture. "Are you okay?"

"Yes, I'm fine," he told her, then added. "I feel her presence."

"I know. Even I feel it. It's throughout this place. Do you think she approves of what we are doing? I mean with the fundraiser and the center?"

"I think she would be very happy."

"I guess we should be going back downstairs."

"Yes," Dale started towards the steps to join her, then stopped. "Wait. What was it you were talking about, the other day, when you said there were other things I didn't know about you?"

"Now's not the time."

"If not now, when?"

Ava paused, checked to see there was no one within hearing distance. "I haven't told you everything."

"Nor I you. I don't expect you to tell me everything. We have only had one date and that one was interrupted."

"If you knew, you wouldn't go out with me."

"Why don't you let me decide that?"

Ava turned away from him and took a deep breath before continuing. "What I didn't tell you was that, when I was in college, I had an abortion." Ava waited for Dale to react.

"Oh," Dale said as he waited for more.

"I was engaged. My fiancé didn't want the baby and talked me into it. Then we broke up. I haven't told anyone, not even my family.

No one except Pastor Joe." Saying it again, made it more real. She longed for the stony front she had put on before, in front of Joe. She resisted the tears forming around the corners of her eyes.

"And what did he say?" Dale's kind tone made it even harder to hold back the tears.

"That God forgives even this."

"I believe that."

"Joy never would have done such a terrible thing. She kept her baby even when she knew it might be the end of her," Ava's voice cracked.

"But Joy was much older than you were."

"No, even if she had been in college and not married, she wouldn't have done this. She's stronger than me."

"How do you know this?"

"I just do. From everything people have said about her."

"She was strong. Did you know I wanted her to at least consider having an abortion, but she wouldn't? When her mind was made up, there was no changing it."

"And now I'll have no children of my own. That's God's punishment."

"You really believe that?"

"Yes." Ava tried to wipe away her tears with her finger.

"Then why has God punished me and my children by taking Joy away from us? What did I do wrong? What did my children do wrong?"

"I don't know. I guess I haven't thought of it that way." Ava looked away, not meeting his gaze. Dale paused, looking down at the floor before saying anything more.

"I'm no better than anyone. I'm not in a position to judge. I had suggested Joy have an abortion. Fortunately, Joy was better than me." Dale felt his phone vibrate in his pocket. He figured he knew who it was. "Maybe it's time we go down stairs before they send out a search party for both of us," he said as he searched his pocket for a tissue to wipe away her tears.

"Maybe," Ava said, but she didn't move as she looked up into Dale's eyes.

He moved closer, wiped her tears with the tissue, then placed his hand on her chin and guided her lips toward his.

"Daddy!" Ashley appeared at the bottom of the steps.

Dale and Ava abruptly separated.

"Right here, Ashley. I'm coming," he yelled down the steps. "Do you think she saw anything?" he asked Ava.

"I don't know. You better go down. I'll be down in a minute." Ava moved over to the picture while Dale rushed down the steps.

"What were you doing?" Ashley asked. "Why were you gone so long?"

"Just putting your mother's picture back on the wall." He was relieved when Ashley didn't say anything else.

"Time to go home," he said as they went back into the ball room. He collected Grace and Jacob from Michelle.

"How'd we do?" he asked Esther and Kathleen.

"We've just got some preliminary numbers, but it looks like we made around twenty thousand with an additional ten thousand in pledges. Enough to pay for the boiler. We are on our way," Kathleen said.

"That's good. Any news on Sara?"

"Just that they have admitted her. We are going to the hospital once we are finished here. What about you?" Esther said.

"I've got to get these kids home. Let me know what happens."

Ava remained upstairs long enough to regain her composure. She stood for a while in front of the picture of Joy, as if waiting for some sign that what had just happened was okay.

"I'm sorry about what happened," she finally said. "I'm not as strong as you, or as good as you. I don't deserve someone like Dale."

The picture remained silent as she walked down the stairs.

"It was a good night," Kathleen told her when she came back into the ball room. She gathered the volunteers that remained.

"Thank you so much for all of your work," she told them. "We couldn't have done it without you. I'm so grateful, and I believe Joy would be, too, if she were here."

"She is here," Esther added. "And she approves. Thank you from all of my family and thank you to the board members, especially Ava who orchestrated the decorations and the entertainment."

The group dispersed. Joe took Michelle and Stephanie home; Josh drove Scott and Erick home.

"Ava, you did a great job with the entertainment," Kathleen added her praises to her mother's, taking Ava aside.

"Do you believe that? What you said about Joy?" Ava asked.

"Yes, I do."

"She's kind of larger than life, you know. Hard to compete with a ghost."

"Who's competing?" Kathleen asked.

"No one, I was just saying." Ava blushed.

"Are you interested in my brother?" Kathleen smiled.

"No, of course not … but if I were?"

"I thought you were interested in Joe."

"No, he's my pastor."

"That hasn't stopped others."

"We're just friends."

"So, you and my baby brother," Kathleen was enjoying this. "Tell me about it."

"There's nothing to tell."

"Stop lying."

"Okay, so there is something, maybe, but how do I compete with a ghost?"

"You don't. You can't. Joy wanted Dale to remarry someday, told him so. You can't compete with Joy, so don't try. Just be yourself and if it's meant to be it will happen."

"This coming from the expert on relationships. Whatever she's saying, Ava, don't listen to her," Esther said as she and Peter joined the two. "We are going to the hospital. Are you going to meet us there?" she asked Kathleen.

"Well, I thought about going out and celebrating, but I guess the hospital is as good a place as any. I'll be there once I lock up."

Chapter 36

Esther and Peter joined Mary and Tom in the maternity waiting room.

"Any word?" Peter asked.

"Not yet. It could be tomorrow before the babies are born," Tom replied.

"We probably should go home and get some sleep," Esther said. Mary and Tom agreed, but no one made a move to leave. Kathleen arrived shortly afterwards, running into Pastor Joe in the lobby.

"What are you doing here?" Kathleen asked.

"My girls are home. I'm wide awake, so I thought I would join you, see how Sara was doing," Joe said. "It's nice to be at the hospital for a happy occasion."

"I couldn't sleep either so I figured if I were going to be up, I might as well be here."

When they reached the waiting room, the four were slumping in their chairs, half asleep.

"My, you're a lively group. Where's the party? I thought this was a celebration," Kathleen said.

"No word yet. Just trying to get a little shut-eye," Peter said. "Joe, what brings you?"

"I heard there was a party," he smiled. "Just thought it would be nice to be here for a happy occasion rather than an emergency. Besides, Sara and Larry are still part of my flock. You forget, I married them."

"It is nice for a change after the last few visits to the hospital," Esther agreed.

"Anybody up for Euchre?" Peter pulled out a deck of cards.

"Let's get this party started," Kathleen said. "Where do we get snacks?"

"That will be the vending machines outside of the cafeteria. The cafeteria is closed for the night," Joe told her as Esther, Mary and Tom paired up for a game of Euchre. "I'll show you."

"It was a good night," Kathleen commented as they rode down in the elevator.

"It sure was. So, are you and Patrick an item?" Joe asked.

"Patrick? No. He didn't know many people at the event so I kept him company. Besides, he and his dancers performed at no cost."

"Was that the case with the saxophone player as well?"

"What were you doing, spying on me all night?"

"No, but I couldn't help but notice."

"Sure you could have, but you didn't."

"I was just wondering."

"And why?" Kathleen turned to confront him.

"Why does everything have to be a fight with you?" Joe met her angry gaze.

"I didn't start it. Why does everything have to be an interrogation with you?"

"Look, we had a good night. This is a celebration, let's not ruin it." They both turned back to face the elevator door.

"And what about you and Ava?"

"I told you before, it's nothing. And I didn't spend the night hanging onto her every word like you did with that Irishman."

"You're right. This is a celebration so let's not ruin it. Let's just get the snacks and get back upstairs," Kathleen said as they stared at the elevator doors waiting for them to open.

"This elevator takes forever," Joe commented.

"What right do you have to question me about who I spend time with?" Kathleen turned back to face him. "You aren't even my pastor."

"You're right. I have no right. I have no right to be here either. Maybe I should just leave." Again Joe met her glare.

"Maybe you should."

"Is that what you want?"

"Only if that's what you want."

"Kathleen, why do you have to be so infuriating?"

"Only because you infuriate me." Kathleen looked at him with flames in her eyes. Before she knew it she was being held in a warm embrace, his lips meeting hers in a kiss. Kathleen found herself responding to his touch, only to be interrupted by the elevator door opening. They were embarrassed by two orderlies who just smiled and let them off. They rounded the corner to the cafeteria.

"That was embarrassing," Kathleen stated once she saw they were alone again.

"Yes it was … and exhilarating," Joe agreed.

"It was. Maybe we should try it again." This time Kathleen pulled him towards her in a firm embrace, kissing him full on the lips and rubbing her fingers through his hair. There was the slight feel of stubble on his cheeks.

"Now this is a celebration," she laughed as their lips separated long enough for her to speak.

"My kind of celebration." Joe's lips met hers as they both laughed and kissed until interrupted by Kathleen's phone.

"Let it go," Joe said as they continued to kiss. Kathleen reached down to see who it was.

"My mom. They must have news about Sara," Kathleen said as she answered. "Okay, we'll be up shortly." Kathleen ended the call.

"They just took Sara into the delivery room. It won't be much longer now. They are wondering where the snacks are."

"I guess we better get back up there," Joe said.

"Yes, we better." They stood together in front of the vending machine checking out the assortment of chips and candies before making their selections. They rode back up in the elevator in silence, neither acknowledging what had happened. Their arms were loaded with snacks, making a repeat of their earlier performance impossible. Joe used his elbow to push the required buttons.

"Here we are," Joe announced as he pushed the door open with his shoulder.

"About time," Peter said. "What took you so long? We were beginning to think you were lost."

"That elevator takes forever," Kathleen avoided her mother's look.

"That it does," Tom agreed.

Chapter 37

Dale's lips burned from that kiss. It was so strange to kiss anyone who wasn't Joy. His lips also burned with guilt.

"What were you and Miss Ava doing, Dad?" Ashley asked on the ride home.

"Nothing, just talking."

"It didn't look like nothing."

"What did it look like?"

"You were standing awfully close."

"I like Miss Ava," Jacob joined the conversation. "Could she be our mother?"

"Whoa, no one's talking about a new mother," Dale said. Ashley remained silent. Grace was asleep in her car seat. "What gave you that idea?"

"Grandma says you should be going out, finding us a new mother," Jacob said.

"Grandma Mary or Grandma Esther?"

"Both. They think you're moping around."

"When did they say this?"

"I heard them say it to each other last Sunday. Said it was time for you to get on with your life."

"And what do you think about that?"

"I would like a new mother."

"I don't," Ashley entered the conversation. "I don't want anyone else in our family. I want it the way it was."

"But that can't be, Ashley. You know that."

"I don't want a new mother," Ashley insisted.

"That's okay, Ashley. Even if I were to remarry, she wouldn't have to be a new mother for you. I know no one can replace your mother. She could just be a friend. Would that be okay?" Ashley refused to answer.

As Dale was tucking her in that night Ashley finally spoke, "Daddy, I don't want you to be sad anymore."

"Have I been sad?"

"Yes, you have. You're sad every day. I can tell. I want you to be happy."

"And if going out with someone other than your mom makes me happy?" Again Ashley retreated into silence. Dale kissed her good night, "I love you. You kids make me less sad."

Chapter 38

The first baby, a girl, arrived a little after midnight; the second, a boy, an hour later. When the second didn't arrive immediately after its sibling, Sara was worried, as were the crowd in the waiting room.

"Is something wrong?" Sara asked when told not to push.

"Nothing," the doctor replied, "The baby isn't ready yet. We'll tell you when to push."

"Are you sure the baby is okay?"

"Everything's fine. Give yourself a break, rest. It's not a race. These things take time." The nursing staff cleaned up the baby girl and laid her in Sara's arms to await a second round of pushing.

"She's so beautiful," Larry said to Sara as he cradled their daughter while awaiting the arrival of baby number two, a son. He stayed by her side throughout the labor, only excusing himself long enough to call his parents.

"I'll call you when the babies are born. No sense in rushing here. Sara's parents and other family members are here with us. We are fine," he assured them.

"But I want to be there," Clara, his mother, responded as his dad restrained her.

"Tomorrow will be plenty soon to see our grandchildren," he told her.

Sara was exhausted after the births. When she heard about the crowd still in the waiting room, she smiled through her tiredness. Wiping away tears, she welcomed them as they came into her room to see the babies,

"They are so beautiful," Mary stated. "What are their names?"

"Angela Joy, for Joy, and Gabriel Jacob for our grandfathers," Sara told them.

"Joy would like that," her mom said.

"I can't believe you all stayed up for this," Sara said.

"Why wouldn't we stay up for our newest grandchildren?" Tom asked.

"Remember what I said before. You are both family," Esther told Sara and Larry.

"That's right. You're not getting rid of us," Kathleen added.

"And Pastor Joe," Sara reached for his hand.

"I spend so much time in hospitals for emergencies, you can't deny me the chance to be in on this blessing. And maybe we can talk about baptisms," Joe said.

"We'll talk, but later," Larry said preparing to escort them from Sara's room.

"I think it's time to get some rest, and let you get yours as well," Tom said. He led Mary out but not until they took one last look at the twins.

"You better get some sleep," Sara told Larry, pointing to the cot that had been rolled into the room. Larry looked grateful for the suggestion but hesitated.

"Are you sure you're okay?"

"I've got all of this help at my fingertips," Sara indicated the nurses. "They are taking care of Angela and Gabriel – besides, I need to sleep. I don't want to worry about you." Larry agreed and stretched out on the cot.

"I'm not going anywhere," Sara told him. "Get your rest."

The rest of the group rode down in the elevator together then went their separate ways. Joe's car wasn't far from Kathleen's. He paused as the others pulled out of the parking structure then went over to her.

"You know, what happened tonight ..." he started.

"Don't worry. We were just caught up in the excitement of the moment. It didn't mean anything," Kathleen interrupted him.

"Yeah, that," Joe said. "It won't happen again. The two of us ..."

"I know, ridiculous, right. I don't even attend church."

"Oil and water."

"We just don't mix." They agreed.

"Good night," Joe awkwardly reached out his hand to shake hers.

"I can't date someone who doesn't even attend church," he told himself as he drove home. "What was I thinking?"

"What was I thinking," Kathleen asked herself. "A minister? Like that would ever work? Not with my past. Besides he is so ... good. I don't do good."

As Larry gently snored on the cot, Sara thought about Joy, all the nights she had spent alone in the hospital. "So, this is what it's like, to be in the hospital overnight. At least I'm not alone," she told herself.

So many months of waiting, and now her babies were finally here. One minute it seemed this day would never get here; now that it was here, it seemed like but a minute. Time, that elusive quantity. Time was both friend and foe. Would time bring healing? She wanted healing but she also wanted to hold on to her feelings as a way to hold on to her sister.

"I wish Joy were here," she thought before falling asleep.

Chapter 39

Ava's lips burned as she drove home after the event. She felt guilty for the kiss, for allowing Dale to kiss her, for kissing him back.

"What was I thinking," she asked herself. "A widower with three kids. He deserves better than me. It was just the excitement of the moment," she told herself. She slept fitfully despite how tired she was, woke up and decided she needed to clear her head with a run.

She took her chance running in the woods by Dale's home. The fresh air and nature quieted her spirit as her mind raced.

She had been asked to stay at St. Luke's, but had been offered another position back in Nebraska. It would be more pay and was closer to home. This year had been good, but she missed her family. She was feeling more at peace with herself, more accepting. She didn't need to run away any more, she told herself. Maybe she could go home. Maybe she had accomplished what she was meant to accomplish and it was time to go home. No need to run any longer.

So then what was she running from now? The idea popped unbidden into her head.

"I'm not running away," she told herself, but she didn't believe it.

She was surprised by the same dog she had first encountered last fall, running up to her barking and wagging his whole body.

"Lucky!" a familiar voice shouted.

"Is that you again, Lucky?" Ava stopped to pet him until Dale arrived.

"Lucky, come here," Dale called. "Sorry about that."

"No need to apologize. I like dogs."

Dale approached her. "And about last night ..."

"I'm not sorry about that," Ava said.

"Neither am I." They stood looking down at the ground.

"So, what do we do now?" finally Ava asked.

"I don't know. It's been so long since I've dated anyone. Maybe coffee?" Dale raised his eyes to meet hers.

"You know, I've been offered a teaching position back in Nebraska, a good one, better pay and benefits."

"Oh, are you going to take it?"

"I don't know. I haven't decided."

"Well, don't let me get in the way."

"You aren't in the way."

"Then, what am I?"

"I don't know. Maybe someone I may like?"

"And maybe I like you." Dale moved closer to her. "What are you running from?"

"I don't know."

Dale stepped even closer and kissed her like the night before. "Hey, I'm not asking for a lifetime, just a cup of coffee," he said as they kissed again.

"Yes," Ava said, "To the coffee that is."

Chapter 40

"Where'd you go last night?" Stephanie asked the next morning over breakfast.

"To the hospital to see Sara's babies."

"She had her babies. What did she have? Why didn't anyone tell me?" Michelle asked.

"A boy and a girl, Gabriel and Angela."

"You don't usually go to the hospital for babies," Stephanie commented.

"That's because I don't usually know about babies until the parents want them baptized. I don't usually get called to the hospital unless it's an emergency."

"So why did you go last night?"

"Why are you so full of questions?"

"Just curious, I guess." They ate their cereal in silence for a while.

"Why don't you date?" Stephanie broke the silence.

"What brought that on?"

"I just wondered. It's been years since Mom died and you haven't dated anyone. Aren't you lonely?"

"With you two around?"

"I'm serious, Dad. Why don't you date?"

"I'm serious, too. Two women in my life are all I can handle."

"Ha, ha, Dad," Stephanie rolled her eyes.

"Okay, maybe because I've been so busy with work. Ministry is a pretty all-consuming job."

"Other ministers are married."

"Maybe I haven't found the right woman yet."

"Well, you know, I won't be around forever. One more year and I'll be going to college, and then Michelle. Maybe it's time you start looking for someone or you'll end up old and alone."

Stephanie picked up her spoon and took a bite of cereal.

"What brought this on?"

"I'm just saying. There are plenty of single women in the church who would love to date you."

"I can't date a church member, too complicated."

"Then how about looking outside the church? Scott's mom is single."

"She doesn't go to church."

"You don't date church members, and you don't date people who don't go to church. What's left? Sounds to me like a convenient excuse." Stephanie finished off her cereal and removed the bowl to the sink, picking up Michelle's bowl on the way.

"So, you would be okay with me dating someone?"

"Sure, Dad. You aren't getting any younger."

"I'll take that into consideration," he said as he left the table.

Larry's parents couldn't wait to see their new grandchildren. They arrived around noon with flowers, balloons and stuffed animals.

"Where are my grandbabies?" Clara said as she walked in. She went to the basinet where they were sleeping and picked one up. "Which one is this?"

"I believe that's Gabriel," Larry told her.

"When are you coming home? Do you need any help?"

"Don't know yet," Sara said. "I guess I'll be discharged tomorrow. They don't keep you any longer than absolutely necessary unless you have complications." The thought of being alone with two helpless infants who were dependent on them for everything was overwhelming. "We're going to stay at my mom and dad's for a while until we get adjusted. Just a few days." Larry and she had discussed this earlier that morning.

"Anne's going to be bringing the baby stuff we need from Detroit, along with some extra clothes." Sara hooked her fingers around Larry's hand and looked at him for support. "I guess we'll figure it out as we go, but it's good to know we have family to call on if we need them."

Kathleen felt the need to blow off some steam that next night. She called Letty and made arrangements to go to Delbert's club.

Jerome was happy to see her, as always, but, to Kathleen's surprise, there was no spark this time. Kathleen had been enjoying the flirtation but this time there was nothing. Delbert congratulated her on the success of last night's event.

"Jerome told me you had a full house with full checkbooks."

"It was good."

"Any time you want to quit that establishment and join me, you let me know."

"It wasn't me who pulled it all together. I had a lot of help."

"The sign of leadership. How much they paying you? I'll double it."

"Actually, I haven't been getting paid, but that's changing. Though I'm only being paid for twenty hours a week."

"I'll quadruple your pay. Four times nothing is still nothing, and I'll hire you full time."

"You can't afford me," Kathleen laughed. It was a thought, though. Maybe her work was done. Once she had the Center on a stable financial basis, maybe she could leave. Maybe she could think about herself. Not that she hadn't done that in the past. Back then that was all she thought about, herself. Did she really want to go back to being like that? One more year and Scott would be in college. One more year – she could give it one more year.

"Maybe next year, once the Center is on a stable footing."

"Girl, I know about non-profits. They're always in crisis. They always operate in the red. You'll never leave if that's your plan."

"Not all. Some do operate in the black."

"What foolishness are you talking, old man," Letty joined them. "Don't be listening to Uncle Delbert. The Center can make it. Look at United Way. It's a non-profit."

"And they've always got their hands out for money.

"And you don't? What do you think a business is? You are always asking for money?"

"They are paying for a product, making a purchase."

"It's still money. At least we don't have our hands in other people's pockets," Letty teased.

"Don't you be offering my job to no white woman," Jerome joined the conversation. "No offense, Kathleen."

"None taken."

"I wouldn't be offering your job if you were doing it rather than wagging your tongue."

Kathleen laughed. "I didn't mean to start a family squabble."

"You can't start something that was already begun a long time before you came along," Jerome said. "You want a job. You talk to me. We can always use a smart woman like you."

It was nice to have options, even if you had no plan to exercise those options, Kathleen thought.

Chapter 41

After the fundraiser, the recital would be a piece of cake, Kathleen thought. She had been amazed at how the dinner and auction had all come together in such a short amount of time.

"Just shows you what can be done when you put your mind to something," Peter had said over dinner.

"I don't know. There have been plenty of times in the past when I've put my mind to something and it didn't come together," Esther said.

"Okay, so the timing was right. It was a convergence. Let me have my moment."

"Our moment, Mr. Chairman," Esther smiled and clasped his hand.

They could use the stage in the ballroom and fill the hall with rows of chairs for this year's recital. They would even have room in the back for tables to display and sell art work and other items in support of the Center. Between ticket sales and saving on hall rental, they might actually make money this year. They could use this opportunity to promote their vision for Joy's Center for Healing and the Arts and to get donations and pledges of support.

Kathleen was glad to get back to a slower pace. She had not been able to spend as much time with her clients as she liked because of the demands of her course work and the fundraiser. She was looking forward to a break over the summer. Once the recital was over, the only event was her mom's wedding in July.

She had allotted extra time this Friday to spend with Peter's mom, Nan. She looked forward to their visit. Over the course of the last two years, Nan had become more than a client for Kathleen. She was her first client and a friend and mentor, giving her little tidbits of wisdom to help her through Joy's death and other struggles.

Kathleen had been surprised when no one came to the door when she knocked. Usually Nan left the door unlocked when she knew Kathleen was coming. Kathleen tried the door; it was locked. She tried calling but got no response.

"Peter, something's wrong. Your mom isn't answering her phone or her door."

"I'll be right over." The fifteen-minute wait for Peter seemed to drag on forever.

"Why didn't I take the key she had offered me?" Kathleen chastised herself. Nan had offered her a key a number of months ago. Kathleen had turned it down as unnecessary. She had been concerned that it was not a good precedent to set. She did not want to be put into a position of being accused of anything. Now she regretted that decision.

When Peter unlocked the door, they found Nan on the floor, barely conscious, but breathing. Her Life Alert was left on the night stand.

Kathleen called 911 while Peter tried to wake his mother up. Peter rode in the ambulance while Kathleen followed behind.

"She'll be okay," Kathleen assured herself. She called her mom to let her know what was going on. Esther was at Dale's watching the kids while Mary and Tom spent time in Detroit with their new grandbabies.

"I'll be over as soon as I can arrange for a sitter," Esther told her.

"They think she had a stroke," Peter told Kathleen when he joined her in the waiting room.

"But she's going to make it?"

"They think so, she's stable. They won't know the extent of the damage until they run some more tests. Then she'll require months of rehab and even then she may not regain her full faculties. I don't know that she will be able to live independently anymore." Peter's face showed a tiredness Kathleen had never seen before. He had always been so upbeat. "That will kill her if the stroke doesn't."

"She'll adapt. She always has. She doesn't exactly have a choice. You hungry?" Kathleen asked.

"Well, yeah. I was going to have lunch with your mom."

"They're running tests. There's nothing we can do right now. We might as well grab a bite at the cafeteria." This time it was Kathleen's turn to take care of him.

They walked to the cafeteria from the emergency room. As they passed the vending machines, Kathleen flashed back to that night a few weeks ago. Peter didn't notice anything.

"How like a man," Kathleen thought. "My secret is safe." Her mother would have noticed.

Peter was uncharacteristically quiet as they ate. He ate half of his cheeseburger, then left the rest sitting on his plate.

"You okay?"

"Sure, I'm fine. Why do you ask?"

"I've never seen you not finish a burger."

"Just doesn't taste that good." Peter looked back down at his cheeseburger, started to pick the burger up, then put it back down. "I want to thank you for all you've done for my mom these past two years. Without your help, I don't know if she would have been able to live independently as long as she has."

"It's not like you haven't done anything for my mom. She's never been happier."

"That's as much for me."

"Well, I can say the same about your mom. I've enjoyed spending time with her. She's quite a woman."

"That she is. Did I tell you how she raised us as a single mom after my dad left?"

"You did. Much like my mom raised us."

"Your mom's quite the woman, too."

"So, how was it for you, growing up without a dad?" Kathleen finished the remainder of her meal as he talked.

"I was older than you were when my dad left. I was glad he was gone. He had been a violent drunk. If he hadn't left, I may have killed him."

"I didn't know that."

"It's not something I talk about."

"Does Mom know?"

"Yes, I told her. After Dad's death I was so busy working odd jobs to help support my mom and little brother. Mom worked as a waitress, long hours."

"That must have been hard."

"No harder than many others. It made me the man I am today."

"What happened to your brother?"

"He became an alcoholic like our dad. He was left too much on his own as a child." Peter stared off into space.

"Is that why you became a probation officer?"

"Maybe. It's so long ago. I hardly remember why. I wanted to go into criminal justice, thought I'd join the FBI. When that didn't happen, probation officer seemed like a good route."

"Is your brother still alive?"

"He died ten years ago, cirrhosis of the liver."

"And I thought I had it hard." Kathleen stared down at her plate. "At least I still have my brother."

"We all have our own particular hardships."

"I sometimes wonder if not having a dad has made it impossible for me to ever have a healthy relationship with a man."

"Maybe at first, but there's a point where you have to take responsibility for your own life, not blame others or past circumstances. You truly are in charge of your own destiny."

Kathleen knew it was a cliché, but this time it didn't bother her the way Peter's clichés usually did. Peter pushed his plate away.

"You done? We better get back," he said.

When they got back to the waiting room, Esther and Pastor Joe were waiting for them.

"You again," Kathleen said to Joe. "Do you live here?"

"Some days it feels like it. I dropped Michelle off at your brother's to babysit so Esther could come. Thought I would see if there was anything I could do."

"Have you heard anything?" Esther asked as she hugged Peter.

"Not anything more than what I had already told you. Kathleen and I just finished lunch."

"I'll see what I can find out," Joe told them.

"He can be helpful at times," Kathleen said as Joe walked through the emergency doors.

"Only at times?" Esther asked. Kathleen didn't respond.

"She's back from the tests if you want to go see her," Joe told them when he got back.

"All of us?" Kathleen asked.

"Sure," Joe said, glancing at the nurse's station. "I'll show you to her room."

They crowded into the small room, Joe standing guard by the door. Nan was awake, seemed to recognize Peter, but was unable to speak. The right side of her face drooped and she was unable to form words.

When the doctor arrived, he confirmed what they already knew.

"She's had a stroke. It's a pretty severe one. We'll be keeping her for a few days for observation. Have to make sure she doesn't have another stroke. Then she'll be sent to a rehab facility."

"What's the chance of a full recovery?" Peter asked.

"At her age, not good, but not impossible. Only time will tell. We'll be moving her upstairs as soon as a room is available."

"Thank you, doctor," Peter said to the doctor as he left. "I guess there's no reason for you to stick around," he told Kathleen and Joe.

"I'll stay with Peter," Esther told them.

"Looks like we've been dismissed," Kathleen said as they walked down the hallway.

"I guess we have. Did you want to get something to eat?"

"I just had lunch with Peter."

"Oh, that's right. Coffee?"

"No, I think I'll head home."

"I can walk you to your car." Joe held the door for her as they left the emergency room.

"I can walk myself."

"I didn't mean that. I just thought I'd keep you company. Is this a brush off?"

"No, that would imply a relationship."

"What are you talking about?"

"I'm just not interested in you, don't you get that?"

"I guess I do now. I thought we were friends. We do work together at the Center."

Kathleen caught herself. She didn't know why he irritated her so. They did have to work together. Why complicate matters?

"I guess coffee wouldn't hurt."

"No, that's okay. You made yourself clear. I better get back to the church."

"And I better get back to the Center. See you around." Kathleen climbed into her car and drove away.

Chapter 42

Word had spread quickly about the end of the school year party at Brian's. Stephanie met up with her friends a block away from her home.

"Can't have any of Dad's church members see me and inform my dad," she had explained. They were used to the routine. She hadn't been able to get out for a while; her dad had been keeping a watchful eye on her.

The party was just starting when they arrived.

"Let the party begin," Stephanie announced as they walked in. "Where's the beer?"

Brian's sister, Suzanne, was friends with Scott and his friends. She had begged them to come.

"Please, my lame brother is having a party. I'll be stuck with all these people I don't know if you don't come."

Scott and Roger showed up about nine, when the party was in full swing.

"So, look who we have here," Brian said as they came in. "Nerd patrol."

"Where's Suzanne?" Roger asked.

"Out back with the other nerds." Scott didn't feel he deserved the term. He was far from the braniac the term implied, but wasn't about to argue. He chose to take it as a compliment.

They found Suzanne and their friends outside by a bonfire.

"The house is way too noisy, and it reeks of weed. Brian better hope the smell clears out before Mom and Dad come back on Sunday," Suzanne said. "You want some pop? It's in the cooler on the porch." Suzanne directed them back to the house.

"I'll get some," Scott volunteered. Through the sliding doors on the porch he could see Stephanie, leaning against the kitchen counter, beer in one hand, laughing as a senior he didn't recognize nuzzled her neck. Just what he didn't want to see. He looked into the cooler and picked up a beer despite his best intentions. After all, he wasn't driving tonight.

He brought Roger a pop. "What's up? You being stingy with the beer?" Roger said when he saw Scott's beer can.

"You're the designated driver," Scott commented as he downed the can.

He did not want to see Stephanie again, so he avoided the house, only slipping back to the porch for an additional beer and relieving himself of his first beer against a tree.

"Scott, go further next time," Suzanne complained.

Josh, home for the summer, arrived around ten o'clock with a few of his buddies, in search of other friends.

"I hear there's a party going on," he said with a grin as he opened the door.

"Hey, Josh," Brian welcomed him with a fist bump. "Scott's out back."

"Oh, he is," Josh said. He hadn't been looking for Scott, hadn't expected him to be there, especially since Josh had the car for the night. "That's good to know."

He saw Stephanie, falling over drunk, hanging on to some guy he didn't know, laughing and smoking weed. Was that why Scott was here? Stephanie climbed on a coffee table and started to dance, raising her tight top over her head as everyone watched and cheered her on.

Josh took one look and decided to take action. He pulled her off the table amidst protests and took her out the front door to a wooded area on the side of the house.

"Who do you think you are? My brother?" Stephanie shouted at him as he lowered her to the ground.

"You would be lucky to have me as a brother. I thought you knew better than this, that you were too smart to be so stupid."

"Can't a girl have a good time?" Stephanie snapped at him.

"A smart girl knows the difference between having a good time and making a fool of herself."

"I don't see why you care."

"Where's Scott? Did you drag him here with you?"

"I haven't seen Scott all night. Is that all you care about? Your loser little brother?"

"Yes, and you are no good for him."

"But maybe I could be good for you," Stephanie said as she approached Josh, threw her arms around him and kissed him full on the mouth.

Scott had been going further away this time to relieve himself. He moved to the wooded area and was about to unzip when he heard voices he recognized. He moved closer to hear what was being said. When he looked he saw Stephanie and Josh in full embrace, kissing.

"So that's why you told me she's no good for me," Scott yelled. Josh pushed Stephanie away. "You wanted her for yourself, just as you always want everything." Scott turned and ran towards the fire.

"No, Scott. That's not the way it is," Josh yelled after him. Scott continued running without looking back.

"I'm leaving," Scott told Roger, stopping himself short of landing in the fire.

"So soon?"

"I'm leaving, either you drive me or I'm walking. Either way I'm out of here."

"Okay, okay, just a minute."

"I'm not waiting." Scott took off for the drive way and started walking down the road.

Behind him he heard the sound of police sirens – a signal that the party was about to be raided. He heard people shouting, running, tires screeching as cars began racing down the road.

"Scott, wait. I'll give you a ride home," he heard Josh yelling at him. Scott continued down the road, refusing to acknowledge his brother. As Josh continued to yell, Scott angrily turned to confront him. The glare of headlights was blinding. He raised his right hand as a shield, heard another screech of tires as he felt himself being lifted up and thrown over the trunk of the car and into a ditch.

Chapter 43

"Grandma," Josh was relieved to hear his grandmother's voice. He had called their home number, not sure whether anyone would pick up. His great-grandfather would be in bed, his mom wasn't answering her cell phone. His grandma would be with Peter at either house.

"It's Scott. There's been an accident. You have to come right away."

"Slow down, Josh. Where are you?"

"I'm at the emergency room."

"Is Scott okay?"

"I don't know." Josh fought back tears.

"We'll be right there."

"And will you call Mom? I couldn't reach her."

"I will."

"What's wrong?" Peter asked from the couch where they had been watching a movie.

"Scott. There's been some type of accident. That was Josh on the phone. I don't know what all happened." Esther struggled to maintain her composure. "We have to go."

"I'll drive." Peter jumped up from the couch. "You try to reach Kathleen." They both grabbed coats and hurried out to the car.

"She said she was going to the library to study. She may have turned off her phone." Esther tried to reach Kathleen on her cell.

"Kathleen?" Esther was thankful when she got through.

"What's up, Mom? I see Josh has been trying to reach me. I had my phone off." Esther explained what had happened.

"I'll meet you at the hospital," Kathleen said and hung up.

Josh kept replaying those minutes over and over in his head. "Scott!" he could hear his scream reverberating through his brain as he saw Scott turn around and then saw his body being thrown over the front of a car and landing on the side of the road. He couldn't get the image out of his head.

He remembered running up to Scott, pulling him further away from the road, away from the departing cars, and screaming.

"Help me, someone help me," he had called. In all the noise and commotion, no one heard him. He pulled out his cell phone and called 911 for help.

"My brother's been hit by a car," he said to the operator, barely able to remember the address where he was.

Office Nash was busy rounding up teens at the party when the call came through on his radio about a hit and run victim.

"You go check it out," his sergeant told him. "I'll take care of mopping up here."

It had seemed like hours before Office Nash arrived, even though it had just been minutes. Nash knelt down beside Josh and Scott.

"Is he breathing?" Officer Nash asked.

"Yes, just barely," Josh said.

"Okay, the ambulance is on its way," he said as he felt for a pulse.

The ride in the ambulance to the hospital was a blur.

Kathleen beat Esther and Peter to the hospital. She hugged Josh tight.

"Are you okay?" she asked as he hugged her back.

"Mom, it was awful. I saw it. I saw Scott get hit by the car."

"Is he okay? Have you heard anything?"

A nurse approached them.

"Is my son okay?" Kathleen asked.

"We haven't received an update yet. Is there anyone you want us to contact? Family? Your minister?"

Josh looked at Kathleen, unsure what to say.

"Pastor Joe at St. Luke's. Call him," Kathleen told her. "He knows us." The nurse returned to the nurse's station to make the call as Esther and Peter arrived.

"Any word?" Esther asked as they hugged.

"No, nothing yet," Kathleen responded.

"Are you okay, Josh?" Esther asked. Josh's face was ashen.

"I'll be okay as long as Scott is okay." Peter offered to get drinks. No one took him up on his offer.

Joe had been dosing in his chair in front of the TV when woken by his phone.

"Yes," he responded. "Yes, I know the family. I'll be right there."

Joe was used to these late-night phone calls. It didn't make them any easier. He saw a light under Michelle's door and knocked to let her know he was leaving.

"I've got to go to the hospital." Michelle was used to her dad getting late-night calls as well. She was no longer surprised to meet him coming in the door as she was leaving for school.

"Anyone I know."

"Don't know," Joe lied. No sense in her getting worried until he knew more. "Don't stay up too late," he added.

He wasn't surprised by Stephanie's empty room.

When he reached the hospital, Esther, Peter, Kathleen and Josh were talking to a nurse.

"No change in status," the nurse said as they gathered around her.

"But he's stable?" Kathleen asked.

"He's breathing, but he's in a coma," the nurse explained.

Esther gave Joe a big hug. "I'm so glad you came," she said. "How did you find out?"

"The hospital called," Joe explained. Peter shook his hand, Josh hugged him. He started to hug Kathleen, then extended his hand instead as they sat down.

It wasn't his first vigil with the family of a car accident victim.

"Have you been able to see him?" he asked.

"Not yet. They said not until he is stable," Esther said.

"I'll see about that. Sometimes they will let family in, especially if there is clergy with them." He went back into the emergency room, talked to the on-call chaplain who took the family aside in a small room to discuss procedures.

"I can take you back to see Scott two at a time, but you aren't to interfere in anyway with procedures and if the doctor asks you to leave, you have to leave," she explained.

The chaplain took Kathleen and Josh to see Scott while Joe stayed with Esther and Peter.

"Wasn't that long ago that we were here for your mom, and before her, my dad. We seem to be making a habit of this," Esther commented. "They say troubles come in threes. I hope this is the last visit to the emergency room for a long time."

Scott looked natural lying on the table, despite the monitors attached to his chest and the beeping machines. Any blood from the accident had been cleaned away. Josh was thankful for that. They watched the emergency room staff monitoring Scott's vital signs.

"Can I speak to him?" Kathleen asked.

"Yes, but not for long," the chaplain told her. She approached the table.

"Scott, it's Mom. I just want you to know I'm here. I love you. You have to pull through this," Kathleen said, starting to cry. Josh wrapped his arm around her, not saying a word. He wasn't sure Scott would want to hear anything he had to say. He walked his mom out so his grandmother and Peter could see Scott. They joined Joe in the waiting room.

"Is there somewhere private where I could go?" Kathleen asked Joe.

"There's the chapel. I can show you to it," Joe said looking for an okay from Josh, that he was all right alone. Josh shook his head yes.

"I'll be fine. I'll wait here for Grandma and Peter."

Joe led Kathleen to the chapel and sat next to her for a while. When he started to get up to leave, she put her hand on his to stop him.

"Don't go," she said. He sat back down and waited. "I never told anyone this, but the night Joy died ..."

"Yes," Joe encouraged her to continue.

"I had a dream. No, it wasn't a dream. I don't know what it was, a vision maybe. It was real."

"Tell me about it."

"I saw this man, Jesus, pick up Joy and carry her off." Joe waited for more.

"Did he say anything?" he asked after a while.

"No, he just looked at me."

"Did you say anything?"

"Yes, I asked him, 'what about me?' What a ridiculous thing to say."

"Doesn't strike me as so ridiculous. Anything else?"

"No. At first it was peaceful, but since then, sometimes I just feel so angry."

"What about?"

"I get angry at God for taking her, but I'm even angrier that he didn't take me. Why should Joy die while I live? Joy was so good, and me, well, you know me."

"It wasn't your time."

"Wasn't it? I wonder about that, too. I try not to think too much about it, but sometimes, I can't help it. I'm angry at God for taking my dad when I needed him. And now, if God takes Scott ... Three strikes, Pastor. That would be unforgiveable."

"God doesn't take our loved ones."

"Then what was he doing with Joy?"

"Rescuing her. Freeing her from all the pain she was in. God overcomes death."

"That's not how I see it."

"How do you see it?"

"God gives us life, only to take it away from us and leave our loved ones in pain."

"But what about the peace you experienced?"

"I don't know about that. I can't quite figure it out."

They were interrupted by a nurse.

"News about Scott?" Kathleen jumped up.

"No, I'm sorry, nothing yet. I've come for the pastor. You have a phone call." Joe reached for his cell phone, then realized he had left it at home. He wondered how anyone had known to call him here.

He picked up the phone at the nurses' station.

"Pastor Joe?"

"Yes, how did you know to reach me here?"

"It's Officer Nash. I was at the scene of the accident this evening. When we couldn't get through to you on your cell phone, I thought you might be at the hospital with the family."

"So what is so important that you had to contact me at the hospital?" Joe asked, but had his suspicions.

"Your daughter, Stephanie, is here again. She was at the same party that the Reese brothers were at. She was picked up with a group of other students who had been drinking. Another MIP."

Another "minor in possession." Joe suspected as much. He hadn't wanted to say anything to Josh about it, but thought chances were that Stephanie had been at the party as well.

"Are you going to come pick her up?" Officer Nash asked.

"No," Joe paused before repeating, "No. A night in the drunk tank never killed anyone, and it just might knock some sense into her." Joe turned aside and spoke softly as the staff at the nurses' station looked on.

"You can tell her I said that," he said into the phone.

"That I will, Pastor. How is Scott doing?"

"We don't know yet."

"I know this is a bad time, but we are going to have to ask Josh some questions."

"This is a bad time."

"I'm sorry. Tell the family I'm praying for them."

"That I will."

He saw Esther and Peter being speedily escorted out of the ER and into the waiting room.

"Is something wrong?" he asked.

"We don't know. I think Scott's heart may have stopped. There was a lot of noise. People rushed in and we were told to leave," Esther said.

"Let's pray," Joe said, taking Esther's hand and Josh's while Esther held Peter's.

In the chapel, Kathleen was remembering the sight of Scott on the table with all of the wires. As she remembered in her mind, it suddenly seemed real. She was in the room with Scott, watching as doctors and nurses were rushing about, placing paddles on her son. She wanted to speak, to move closer, but was unable to move. Standing alongside the table, she saw Jesus, the same Jesus she had seen on the night of Joy's death.

"Don't you dare touch him," she tried to shout. "Stay away from my son. Take me, not him," she pleaded with the silent figure. The figure raised his right hand and held it over her son as the doctor told everyone to stand back and said, "Charge." She saw her son's body jump on the table. Then Jesus reached down and touched Scott's chest and his heart started. Jesus held his hand on Scott for a moment longer then slipped away. Kathleen broke into sobs as she knew her son would be okay.

The four remained in silent prayer, heads bowed, until the emergency room door opened and they heard Scott's name called. "Family of Scott Reese," she said.

"Yes," they looked up from their prayer. She came over to them.

"Don't get up," she instructed and pulled up a chair across from them. "Scott's going to be okay. He has some internal damage, a couple of broken ribs. We were concerned about internal bleeding and we did need to use paddles when his heart stopped but they worked. We were able to start his heart back up. He's breathing easily now, and coming out of his coma. We are waiting for further test results and x-rays, but it appears he's out of the woods."

"That's great news," Esther said.

"Are you his mother?" the doctor asked.

"No, Grandmother."

"I'll get his mother. She's in the chapel," Joe hopped up to get Kathleen. When he reached the chapel, Kathleen was wiping away tears.

""Good news," Joe said.

"I know."

"Who told you?"

"I just know. Scott's going to be okay."

Joe waited in case Kathleen wanted to say more before asking, "How do you know?"

"Because I saw Jesus heal my son." Joe didn't ask any more. Her face was calm and radiated peace in the dim light of the chapel.

"Come on. You might be able to see Scott again. The doctor said he's coming out of his coma," he said as he led her out of the chapel.

Chapter 44

Joe took his time retrieving Stephanie from jail.

"At least this way I know where she is," he told himself. After the events of the past night, he was beat and slept late.

"Where are you going now?" Michelle asked when he finally got up and came downstairs dressed for the day. "Are you going to the hospital? I want to go with you. Why didn't you tell me Scott was in an accident? I know Scott. He's my friend, too." News of the arrests and Scott's accident had been all over social media that morning.

"First, I have to get your sister out of jail," Joe said. "We can go see Scott this afternoon, if the doctor lets him have visitors."

Stephanie was contrite when he picked her up. She had heard about Scott's accident. She had a splitting headache and had thrown up repeatedly throughout the night. When Joe found out, he figured leaving her in jail had been his best decision where she was concerned in a long time. "Let someone else clean up after her," he thought.

Despite how miserable she felt, she wanted to see Scott and make sure he was okay.

"I might have been the reason Scott was hurt," she said tentatively on the way home.

"How is that?"

"I was drunk, acting like an idiot. Josh saw me and took me outside to talk to me. Like a fool, I threw myself at him and kissed him. I think Scott saw it. He yelled something at Josh and ran off. That was why he was on that road where he was hit."

"Sounds like you owe both Scott and Josh an apology. Scott isn't the only lucky one here. He's lucky to be alive, and you are lucky that he is alive so you don't have to live with a lifetime of guilt." Stephanie didn't argue with him for once.

Joe reached over and felt her forehead. "Are you sure you're okay? Seems that night in the jail may have finally knocked some sense into you."

"Ha ha, Dad," Stephanie pushed his hand off her forehead.

"Now that's my spit-fire, my Stephanie," Joe said.

Chapter 45

Scott was moved from the emergency room to intensive care for observation. Kathleen refused to leave the hospital, even though she knew he would be okay. As she sat in his room, it felt like sacred space.

Scott didn't remember what had happened at first, as he slowly came around.

"What happened?" he asked.

"You were hit by a car," Kathleen explained.

"Oh," Scott blinked. "So, I'm alive. It was a dream."

"What did you dream?"

"I dreamed I had gone to heaven, but Jesus sent me back. I didn't want to come back."

"Why not? You can't leave me or Josh or Grandma."

"It wasn't about leaving anyone. It was such a beautiful place, so peaceful, and Aunt Joy was there. I wanted to stay."

"I'm glad you came back."

"Grandpa was there, too."

"How could he be? He's still alive."

"No, not Grandpop – Grandpa, your dad."

"How did you know it was Grandpa?"

"I just did. You know these things when you are there." Kathleen shook her head in disbelief.

"Did he say anything?"

"Yes, he told me to tell you he knows and it's all right. He said you would know what he was talking about." Kathleen fought back tears.

"Did he say anything else?"

"Just that he loves you, always has and always will." Kathleen reached for a Kleenex to wipe her face at this. "Hey, I'm sorry, Mom. I thought you would like to know."

"Thank you for telling me." Kathleen attempted a smile.

At this Scott groaned. "Wow, I feel like I've been hit by a car."

"You have been hit by a car. Don't you remember anything about last night?"

"No, just that there was a party. Josh was there, and Stephanie ... I don't remember anything else."

"That's enough for now. Get your rest," Kathleen told him. Josh had told her the events of the night. Better if Scott doesn't remember, at least not right away. Plenty of time for that later – tomorrow was another day. As for herself, she remembered the conversation with her mom when she had returned home over four years ago, remembered telling Esther how her last words to her dad had been that she hated him, remembered her mom's words of reassurance that her dad knew she loved him and her own disbelief. She continued to fight tears at the remembrance and Scott's words to her.

When Joe arrived that afternoon with Michelle and Stephanie, Kathleen didn't think it was a good idea for them to visit.

She was with Esther, Peter and Josh in the family waiting room. They had gone home to get some sleep and check on Grandpop before coming back. He still wasn't strong enough to get around that well on his own. The pacemaker and stent had been successfully placed and he was feeling more like his old self, but still weak. He had wanted to see Scott but had been talked out of it.

Esther and Peter were going to Dale's to watch the kids so he could come up and see Scott. Mary and Tom were in Detroit at Sara's and unavailable. Esther and Peter had already gone in to see Scott. He had been sleeping so they left without waking him up.

The nurses were restricting visitors to no more than two at a time.

"Stephanie and Michelle just wanted to see how Scott was doing," Joe explained. "We won't stay long."

"Only family is allowed," Kathleen said, glaring at Stephanie. "I'll see if he's up to seeing anyone." Kathleen was in mother bear mode, protecting her cub.

Stephanie looked over at Josh, then looked at the floor.

"Hey," she said as she walked over to him. "I'm sorry about what happened last night," she said quietly.

"Yeah, sure," Josh responded.

"Thank you for helping protect me from myself."

"Yeah, well, see where it got us." Josh refused to meet her gaze. When he had seen Scott earlier that morning, Scott hadn't remembered anything about that night. Scott had recognized him and smiled, but hadn't said a word. Josh dreaded his remembering, didn't want to remember himself, but he couldn't forget. The events of that night kept whirling around in his brain. Stephanie, trying to talk some sense into her, the kiss, the look on Scott's face, his running away, talking to the police later that night.

"I'm sorry, I don't remember the car. It was dark. All I was thinking about was Scott. I do know that it was a standard model, not a Suburban or SUV. It was a dark color, not white, but other than that, that's all I remember."

"Call us if you remember anything else about that night," Officer Nash handed Josh his card then looked over at Esther and Peter. "Can we talk to Scott?"

Joe had intervened, "He's just coming out of his coma and doesn't remember anything. We'll call you when he is ready to be interviewed."

Josh kept replaying it in his mind, thinking about everything he could have done differently, as if he could somehow magically change the outcome. He had gone home with his grandma, but hadn't been able to sleep as his brain kept him awake. The last person he wanted to see was Stephanie.

Stephanie rejoined her dad and sister.

Scott was awake and sitting up when Kathleen went back to his room.

"Stephanie and her sister and dad are here," she told him. "Do you want to see them?"

"Yeah, sure, send them in," he said with a smile.

They approached cautiously after getting the okay to visit. The nurse made an exception to the two-person rule, as long as they didn't stay too long.

"He's doing quite well," his nurse had said. "We may be moving him to step down tonight or tomorrow, if he continues to do well."

Scott smiled at Stephanie, acknowledging her first, then nodding at Michelle and Joe.

"Hey, Stephanie, Michelle, Pastor Joe."

"It's good to see you doing so much better," Joe said.

"I heard you were here last night," Scott responded. "Thank you." He looked back at Stephanie.

"I think maybe Stephanie has something to say to Scott," Joe said to Michelle. "Right, Stephanie? We'll see you, Scott." Joe led Michelle out of the intensive care unit, leaving Scott and Stephanie alone.

"Hey," Stephanie said again, sitting down alongside of him.

"Hey to you, too. I didn't expect to see you here."

"After what happened last night, I had to see you, see if you were okay."

"I'm glad to see you, too."

"You don't remember what happened, do you?"

"Not really. The doctor said that was common with trauma. The memory will come back as I get stronger. What happened?"

"I was acting like an idiot. Josh tried to stop me."

"I remember being at the party, and I remember Josh yelling at me to stop before I was hit," Scott said.

"It wasn't Josh's fault," Stephanie said.

"What wasn't his fault?"

"The kiss. Josh didn't kiss me, I kissed him. He pushed me away as soon as I did it. I was drunk, didn't know what I was doing."

"Oh," Scott thought. "Was that what I saw?" He was slowly remembering.

"Don't you remember? You saw me kissing Josh, then you ran off and got hit by a car? I'm so sorry," Stephanie cried.

Scott took it all in, putting pieces together. He remembered the kiss, yelling at Josh and running, but in light of the events of the night, it no longer seemed important.

"It's okay, Stephanie," he told her.

"No, it's not," she said. "You can't let me off so easily. Get angry, yell at me."

"No, it's all right. It's not your fault. I was the one who ran off down the street. You didn't make me."

"But what about the kiss?"

"You know, we aren't meant to be. I see that now. You never felt about me the way I felt about you. You can't help that."

"But ..." Stephanie started.

"No, it was my fault. But I would like it if we could be friends again. No pressure, no strings attached."

Stephanie wiped away her tears. "Yeah, I would like that, too." They talked for a while about school, their friends, as if the past months had never happened, until Stephanie was escorted out by the nurse.

She joined her dad and sister in the waiting room. Esther and Peter had gone, leaving Kathleen and Josh.

"I'm really, really, sorry about what happened last night." Stephanie approached Kathleen. "I know you probably hate me. I know you think I'm no good. I've been an idiot. But I want you to know I'm going to try to be better."

Kathleen remained silent. She knew the "right" thing to do was to accept Stephanie's apology, say it was okay, but she was never big on doing the "right" thing. Even after the events of the night, she couldn't accept Stephanie's apology. Even though she knew Joe was watching. She turned away from Stephanie's outstretched hand. Josh took it instead, without saying a word.

Joe took his daughter and led them out of the waiting room. "I think it's time we leave."

Dale showed up just as they were leaving.

"Can I see Scott?" he asked.

"Sure, if he's not too tired," Kathleen said. Dale knew his way around the intensive care unit. He went back by himself to Scott's room.

"I will never forgive her for what she did to my son," Kathleen vented once Dale was gone. "You may forgive her, but I won't," she told Josh.

Scott was still sitting up when Dale arrived.

"You look tired," he said.

"Yeah, well, it feels like I've been hit by a car … oh, wait, I was," Scott joked.

"I won't stay long." Each visit to the hospital brought back memories of visits with Joy, but now those memories were being replaced by new memories, or not replaced, but added to. The old memories were being pushed to the side by new ones. It wasn't quite as hard as that trip to the hospital after Jacob's fall. It was hard, but in a different way. It was hard because his nephew had been in a car accident, but not because of memories searing through his brain, memories of Joy. Those memories were fading some, as new memories came to the forefront. The same thing had happened after his grandfather's heart attack. It's never easy, seeing a loved one in the hospital. Each event was different, evoking its own set of feelings.

"I saw Stephanie on her way out of the hospital. So, how did that go?"

"It went okay. We're friends again."

"Just friends?"

"You know, Uncle Dale, I thought it was like you and Aunt Joy. That eventually Stephanie would come around, but now I realize we are just friends, and that's okay."

"I'm glad you are okay with it."

"So am I."

Chapter 46

Joe, Stephanie and Michelle drove in silence for a while. Michelle hadn't known what to say while in the hospital, especially the intensive care unit. She had seen the patients in other rooms, hooked up to machines. She had been afraid that Scott would be hooked up, too.

"Dad …" she said from the back seat.

"Yes, Michelle."

"You go to the hospital a lot, don't you?"

"Yes, I do."

"I don't like it there."

"It's not for everyone."

"What was it like when Mom died?" she asked. "Was she on machines like those people I saw?"

"No, she died instantly at the scene of the accident. The doctor assured me she felt no pain."

"Did you get to see her?"

"Yes, I got to see her in the Emergency Room after they had cleaned the blood away."

"Was it like on the TV shows?"

"Would you stop asking stupid questions? Mom is gone. Nothing will bring her back," Stephanie snapped.

"I just wanted to know. We never talk about her."

"Maybe there's a good reason for that," Stephanie said.

"Why do you say that, Stephanie?" Joe asked.

"Because I heard you fighting the night of Mom's accident. She wanted a divorce. She was going to leave us anyway. She didn't love us anymore."

"That's not true," Joe said.

"Then she wasn't going to get a divorce?"

"No, that was true. But that didn't mean she didn't love you. She always loved you, both of you girls. She wasn't leaving you, she was leaving me."

"Whatever. She left us anyway. It would have been the same. She was trying to get away from us."

"Why would you say that?"

"Because she said so. I heard her talking to Grandma about how she wished she could get away, escape from everything. That included us."

Joe pulled over to the side of the street so he could face Stephanie.

"Stephanie, I never knew you thought this. Your mom was struggling. She was having a hard time. She was depressed and I wasn't a lot of help. She felt overwhelmed at times with being a mother and a pastor's wife, but she never would have left you. She may have felt like running away, but just for a moment."

"But she did run away, Dad. She ran away and left us forever."

"But we still have each other."

"It's not enough. I miss Mom. I miss having a mom to talk to about all my problems. To ground me when I'm out of line, like my other friends' moms. To argue with me, to shop with me, to help me with make-up."

"I guess I'm not very good at those things."

"You're okay, Dad. You do your best, but you're not Mom."

"No, I'm not. No one can take the place of your mother." Joe reached over the bucket seats and took her hand. He tried to hug her as he heard a voice from the back seat of the car.

"What about me? I lost a mother, too."

"I know you did." Joe reached back to touch Michelle's hair. "My beautiful baby girls. I wish I could make it up to you. I wish there was something more I could do for you."

"You could get this car home and off the street so no one can see this freak show," Stephanie said, wiping away her tears.

"That I can do." They finished the ride in silence. Once inside, Joe didn't try to continue the conversation. The moment was gone and couldn't be forced back.

"So, are you and Scott friends again?" Joe asked over dinner that night.

"I think so, but not if his mom has anything to do with it."

"She'll come around. Give her time."

Chapter 47

Scott had managed to talk his mom into going home that night.

"I'll be fine, Mom. I've got good drugs to knock me out. You don't have to worry about me. I don't want to worry about you staying up another night."

Kathleen slept hard, then was up early with the rest of her family.

"You going to Sunday services?" Esther teased.

"No, you go to your church. I'm going to spend the morning with Scott."

Scott was still sleeping when she arrived. She slipped into a chair and reviewed the text book from her class while he slept.

"Mom?"

Kathleen looked up from her book. She hadn't noticed that he was awake.

"Yes."

"Do you know who my dad is?"

"Oh, what brought this on?"

"I've been wondering for some time, it just never seemed like the right time to ask." Kathleen moved to Scott's side.

"No, I don't. That was not a good time in my life. I was pretty messed up, slept with a few men. I know that's not what you want to hear, nor is it what I want to say. I wish I could tell you more."

"That's okay. That's pretty much what Josh had said."

"You and Josh have talked about this?"

"Yes, he told me to leave it alone, but it's hard to do that. I can't help wondering."

Kathleen took his hand. "Scott, I grew up without a father. I know how tough that can be. Kids used to tease me on the playground."

"They did that to me, too, until Josh took care of them."

"Josh is a good brother."

"Sometimes."

"The last thing I ever wanted to do was to have my children grow up without a father, and yet that is what happened. I was so caught up in my own little world. I didn't think about anybody but myself. I never thought about how hard it would be for you boys. I figured you were better off with Grandma and Great-Grandpa, but I've come to regret those days so much."

"Sometimes it was hard, but Uncle Dale was around a lot when we were little and Grandpop. They were like fathers to me."

"Not the same."

"No, but that's okay. Our family may not look like other families, but it's still ours. I wouldn't trade it."

"Not for a perfect nuclear family with mom and dad and two-point-three kids?"

"Nah, that would be boring."

"You know, I spent my life feeling resentful that I didn't have the picture-perfect family I thought I needed, deserved. And here you are at sixteen, smarter than me, already knowing what it has taken me forty years to learn."

"Some people are just slow learners," Scott teased.

"Or hard headed."

"That too."

"So," Kathleen changed the subject. "What's up with you and Stephanie?"

"We're friends again."

"After all she did to you? The way she treated you?"

"Yeah, well she hasn't exactly had it easy either, losing her mom and all."

"Well, I'll never forgive her for what she did to you. She almost got you killed."

"I think I did that to myself."

"With her help."

"Naw, you give her too much credit. I'm capable of making my own mistakes."

"That you are," Kathleen smiled. "Stephanie reminds me of myself when I was her age. That's not a good thing."

"You turned out okay."

"Yeah, but I hurt a lot of people along the way."

"I'll be okay."

"Seems your choices in women aren't much better than my choices in men." Scott threw his pillow at Kathleen as she laughed. It was good to see how relaxed Scott was. Must be the pain meds, she thought.

Chapter 48

"I think my dad likes your mom," Stephanie told Scott.

"What are you talking about?"

Scott had been kept for observation for a couple of days then had been released on Tuesday with bandages around his chest and instruction to take it easy for a while. Easier said than done. The car that hit him hadn't been going that fast. At least that was how the doctors explained his recovery. The police had interviewed him while he was in the hospital, but he didn't remember anything about the car.

"That's okay, son. There were plenty of people around at that party. We'll find who did this," the interviewing office had said. Scott wasn't interested in that. He just wanted to get home and back to his normal life. Later that week the police had been able to find the students and charged them with leaving the scene of an accident.

"Typical male. You just don't notice, do you? Don't you see the way they avoid each other?" Stephanie said.

"Because they don't like each other."

"No, it's sexual tension. It's in the air around them."

Scott didn't respond. It was good to be friends again with Stephanie, but now he knew it was only friends. They spent alternate days at each other's homes. Now that school was over, Scott was busy working at his uncle's most days. Stephanie had gotten a job as a salesclerk at the mall. Neither was working today so they were spending it at a lake, along with Michelle.

"You take Michelle with you, or you don't go at all," her dad had insisted.

"Okay," Stephanie agreed. Michelle was happy to get out of the house. She came back from swimming and flopped own on the blanket with them.

"You're getting us wet," Stephanie complained.

"Then don't hog the blanket," Michelle responded. "What are you two talking about?"

"Getting Scott's mom and our dad together." Michelle was already informed about Stephanie's desire to find someone for their dad. They had talked about it at times.

"Give Dad something else to occupy his time besides us," Stephanie had explained to Michelle.

"Then you and Josh would be our stepbrothers," Michelle said.

"I hadn't thought about that," Stephanie said. "Let's see if we can even get them in the same room before we worry about that."

"That would be fun," Michelle continued.

"You think so?" Scott asked.

"I always wanted a brother. So what's the plan?"

"Haven't got one yet, but I will," Stephanie said.

Chapter 49

The summer was going by pleasantly for Dale. He had had that coffee with Ava, which led to dinner, then a movie and now they were officially dating. She had helped with Grace's fourth birthday party, and was accepted by the kids, although grudgingly by Ashley. Ava had turned down the position in Nebraska and was staying at St. Luke's.

"It seems I've got unfinished business here," Ava said.

"I hope it's never finished." Dale planted a kiss on her lips.

They had acknowledged the anniversary of Joy's death with a ceremony of remembering at the tree they had planted last year on the first anniversary of her death. Ava joined them for the ceremony, honoring their memories as her own.

The rehearsal dinner for Esther and Peter's wedding was being held at Dale's.

"You've got that big back yard. Nothing fancy. A barbecue would work. We could put up a big canopy and borrow tables and chairs from the church," Esther told Dale.

"Wait a minute, Mom. How many people are you expecting?"

"Just you and your family, and Ava, Kathleen and the boys, Grandpop, Pastor Joe and his girls and Peter's daughters and their families. Oh, and we wanted to invite Larry and Sara if they come early and then Mary and Tom, of course."

"So around twenty people?"

"About."

"I think we can get by without a canopy. If it rains, we'll eat inside. I've got table space and chairs for over twenty people from all of those Thanksgivings we've hosted. Don't worry about a thing. Ava will help me. We'll take care of everything."

"Oh, and Howard. He's family, too."

"Invite Howard. Can't have a family party without him."

Joe wasn't sure about attending the rehearsal dinner. He was always included in the rehearsal as the minister, but he usually didn't attend the dinner afterwards unless he was a friend of the family.

"We're friends, Dad. We want to go," his daughters insisted.

"Okay." He figured he would put in an appearance but not stay long. Joe made a point of avoiding Kathleen, much as she avoided him. The girls could get a ride with Scott if he left early. Despite Stephanie's urgings, he still hadn't gotten her a car.

"I could take Michelle to her dance lessons and run errands for you," she had argued.

"We can't afford it," he insisted, though getting Stephanie to and from her job at the mall was a challenge. On days he couldn't drive her, she rode her bike.

"I'll be the only senior without a car," she complained.

"I highly doubt that's the case."

"Okay, so maybe there will be two or three other seniors without cars."

Only one more year till college, he thought. "I'll never survive it," he said to no one in particular.

Since that morning in May, Stephanie hadn't brought up him dating again. He was relieved, but also a little disappointed. His love life continued to be non-existent. He had tried dating two different women, not from his church but from other churches. It just didn't go well. There was no spark. He didn't know what he was looking for, but it wasn't that.

Kathleen came early to Dale's the afternoon of the dinner with a large bowl of potato salad she had promised her mom to bring. She had bought it at a local deli, then added a few ingredients and poured it into a bowl to give it a home-made appearance.

"What's this?" Grandpop asked when he saw the deli containers in the garbage.

"Nothing, old man, you stay out of this," Kathleen told him.

"If your mom knew ..." he started.

"But she doesn't and you won't tell her."

"You know how your mom is about her potato salad."

"Then she should have made it herself. Besides, this is just as good. Here, try some." Kathleen gave her grandfather a spoonful.

"Hmmmm, not bad. Be careful or you'll get the job of bringing potato salad to all of our family gatherings."

The rehearsal went smoothly. Kathleen was the maid of honor, Peter's oldest daughter the best woman, Jacob the ring bearer, and this time Grace was the flower girl. Esther and Peter hadn't wanted a large bridal party. Dale was going to walk his mom down the aisle. Erick had gladly relinquished this role to Dale, preferring to already be seated with his walker next to him before everyone arrived. Josh and Scott were ushers. Stephanie and Michelle hung out in the back of the church.

"Dad, can we please take the car? We promised Ava we'd come early and help her." Stephanie asked.

"How will I get there?"

"You can ride with Mom," Scott said. "She doesn't have anyone riding with her." Scott and Josh were taking their grandpop in his car.

"We'll be done shortly. You can wait," Joe said.

"That's why we have to leave right now," they insisted.

"Come on, Mom. You can give pastor a ride, can't you?" Scott asked Kathleen.

"I guess," Kathleen agreed.

"There. It's settled." Stephanie and Michelle took the car keys from their dad and left.

"Well, that was pretty obvious," Joe said on the ride over.

"Oh, the maneuvering to get us in the same car? Yeah, what are they thinking?" Kathleen kept her eyes on the road but she couldn't help noticing how Joe looked in his polo shirt and khakis, not the usual pastor garb.

"Like all it would take is for us to spend some time together alone. I'm afraid my daughters are trying to set me up. They think I'll be lonely when they are gone."

"Will you be?"

"The peace and quiet might be nice."

"But are you?"

"Lonely? Who isn't in this life at some time or another?"

"Why do you have to turn a simple question into a mini-lesson?"

"Sorry, just being myself. I'm sorry I'm so annoying to you. I'll make sure I have a ride home."

"I'm sorry, too. This is a happy occasion. Let's not fight." They rode in silence for a while until Joe broke the silence.

"What happened?"

"What do you mean, what happened?"

"I thought there was a spark, back then, after the fundraiser, in the elevator."

"We both agreed it was a mistake."

"Was it? A mistake, that is."

"We have nothing in common."

"For two people with nothing in common, we seem to be spending a lot of time in the same vicinity, avoiding each other."

"That's just work."

"And family."

"I'm not good at relationships. You should know that."

"My track record isn't great either."

"Don't you think it might help if one of us knew what we were doing?"

"We can help each other," Joe suggested.

"Or, hurt each other."

"That too."

Kathleen pulled into the driveway at Dale's. "Look, we can at least be civil, get along, for my mom's sake."

"I'll do you one better. I'll do it for my own sake. Friends?" Joe extended his hand.

"Friends." Kathleen accepted his hand.

"See," Stephanie nudged Scott as Kathleen and Joe exited the car smiling. "I told you. We just had to get them together."

"But will they stay together?" Scott said as they went separate ways, Kathleen going to the kitchen to help Ava and Joe to the back yard.

The sun was out, but not hot and muggy. It was the perfect night for a barbecue. Dale was grilling hamburgers, brats, and hotdogs, while Ava set the table with paper products, condiments, bags of chips and pretzels, Kathleen's potato salad, and veggies and dip. There was watermelon and brownies for dessert.

The evening passed quickly with children running underfoot, the teens playing badminton, while the adults talked.

"Time to head for home," Joe said as the sun set and the party broke up. "Got a big day tomorrow," he grinned.

"Dad, do we have to go? It's still early." Stephanie and Michelle had moved onto the porch where they were playing cards with Josh and Scott.

"How will you get home?"

"I can drive them," Josh offered.

"What about me?" Erick spoke up.

"You're coming home with me, Grandpop," Kathleen said. "I'm ready to go."

"Wait," Stephanie said. "Couldn't your grandpop get a ride with Uncle Howard? Then Dad could ride with your Mom and we could have the car."

"Not going to work this time, young lady." Joe took the keys from Stephanie. "I need the car in case I get called out on an emergency." Joe turned to Josh, "Get them home at a decent hour."

"I will, Pastor."

Just then they heard Ashley yelling for Lucky.

"What's wrong?" Kathleen asked, coming down from the porch.

"It's nothing," Dale said. "Ashley can't find Lucky."

"It's not nothing, Dad. Lucky has never run off like this before," Ashley insisted.

"We'll go look for him in a minute," Dale told her.

"What if he's lost or hurt?"

"I can help look," Kathleen offered.

"It's a lot of woods to cover if he doesn't come back on his own," Dale said.

"I'll help, too," Joe added.

"Josh, Scott, someone has to take Grandpop home."

"Why don't we continue our game at your house?" Stephanie suggested.

"That's fine. We don't need all of you to find one dog. I won't be late," Kathleen told them.

Ava stayed with Grace and Jacob while Dale and Ashley, and Kathleen and Joe, set out in pairs with flashlights to look for Lucky.

"You two follow the path to the right," Dale instructed. "Ashley and I will go on the other path." They separated, following the different paths. "Don't worry, Ashley. Lucky probably spotted a squirrel or rabbit and followed it into the woods. We'll find him," Dale reassured her.

"This is not how I thought this evening would end, in the woods with you," Joe joked.

"Shhhh, we have to listen for Lucky." Kathleen called out for Lucky then listened for a responding bark or the rattle of his dog tags. Nothing.

"These woods go on for miles. I hope you know your way around them."

"I don't. Joy was the one who knew these woods. As long as we stay on the path, we should be okay." Kathleen kept moving forward, leading the way with the flashlight. "If we don't find that dog, Ashley will be devastated. As hard as Joy's death was for the kids, I think having Lucky around helped Ashley deal with it. I don't know what she would do if we don't find him."

"We'll find him," Joe insisted.

"Why do these terrible things keep happening?" Kathleen asked.

"What terrible things are you talking about?"

"Joy's death, Grandpop's heart attack, Peter's mom's stroke, Scott's accident, now Lucky missing."

"There have been good things, too. Sara's babies, your mom getting married, Scott and Stephanie getting along again, the Center."

"But is it enough? So much hurt. I think it was easier back when I was in jail. No one to worry about but myself."

"But was it better?"

"No, I guess not. I missed out on so much when I was locked up. Josh and Scott growing up. I don't know how they were able to forgive me, but they did." Kathleen was surprised as tears surfaced.

"Another blessing. Forgiveness is one of the greatest blessings." The moon broke out from behind a cloud, briefly lighting their way, lighting up Kathleen's face.

"Do you always have to talk in sermons?"

"I'm sorry if you think I've been preaching at you. I don't mean to."

"No, it's okay. You are right. Forgiveness is a blessing."

"Have you forgiven yourself yet?"

"Don't know. I guess I haven't given it much thought. I don't usually like to think about such things."

"Not many people do."

"Maybe I have. I know I'm not as angry as I used to be. I used to feel like I would explode, had to explode. Not anymore." Kathleen paused in her tracks and peered into the darkness, listening again for Lucky.

"You know, I don't think I'm so angry at God any more. I think I've forgiven him," she added.

"Mighty big of you, forgiving God," Joe smiled.

"You know what I mean."

"I think I do."

Kathleen looked out into the darkness. The gaping hole that had always been a part of her was gone. She didn't know exactly when it had happened, but sometime over the past months, between her grandfather's heart attack and Scott's accident, she had been healed. All the anger she had carried, all the resentments that had plagued her, they no longer seemed important. She had let them go. She was no longer that hurt, angry little girl with a hole in her heart. That hole had been filled by the love of so many good people, including Joy, who was present in these woods.

"Shhhh. Do you hear something?" In the distance they heard the clink of something metallic and a whimper.

"It's coming from that direction," Joe pointed.

"Lucky!" Kathleen called and heard a weak bark.

"It sounds like he's hurt," Joe said as they rushed forward. They found him tangled in some wire fencing. Kathleen called Dale as Joe gently pulled the wire away from around Lucky's front paw.

"Where are you?" Dale asked.

"I don't know. There appears to be an old wire fence."

"That's the property line. Is Lucky okay?"

"I don't know yet. Joe's trying to disentangle him. Wait, he's got him out." Lucky kept licking Joe's face as he worked to free him. Once set free, Lucky jumped on him.

"He looks okay, though he's limping some. We'll head back and meet you at your house." Kathleen turned off her phone.

"They found Lucky and he's okay," Dale told Ashley as she hugged him.

Lucky led the way back, limping as he went.

"They'll have to get that foot checked if he doesn't stop limping, but other than that he appears to be okay. I'm just glad we don't have to carry him."

"Too much for you, Pastor?" Kathleen smiled.

"I was thinking of you, since it is your brother's dog," Joe returned her smile. Lucky seemed to feel better the more he walked and the closer he got to home. Kathleen and Joe had to walk fast to keep up.

"Slow down, boy," Joe said as Lucky took off at a run, leaving them behind.

"I think he's just fine," Joe turned to look at Kathleen. "You doing okay? You look winded."

"I'm fine, too."

"You know," Joe stopped her. "I was just thinking. If you are no longer so angry at God, do you think you could stop being so angry at me?"

"Is that what you think I've been doing?"

"It does happen. You tell me."

"I thought it was just that you are so normally annoying."

"Is that so? That's the only reason you can't stand me?"

"I didn't say that."

"So maybe you can tolerate me?" Joe took her hand.

"Maybe," she said, not withdrawing her hand from his as they walked the remainder of the path to Dale's backyard.

Chapter 50

The wedding was beautiful, replete with crying babies and Grace refusing to walk down the aisle with Jacob, clinging to Dale as he escorted his mother down the aisle. The church hall was decorated simply with wild flowers. Esther hadn't wanted to make it a big production since this was a second wedding for both of them.

"But there will be music and there will be dancing," Esther insisted.

Esther and Peter waltzed gracefully together in their first dance as husband and wife.

"All those ballroom lessons paid off," Kathleen said to Dale.

When family members were invited to join them on the floor, Dale and Kathleen tried dancing together.

"Maybe we should have taken advantage of those dance lessons, too," Kathleen said as Dale stumbled and landed on her toes.

"You think," he said. They were rescued by Joe and Ava as other dancers were invited onto the dance floor. Jacob, Ashley and Grace were sliding across the floor together. Michelle and Stephanie watched Angela and Gabriel so Larry and Sara could dance.

"Thanks for rescuing me," Kathleen told Joe. "I love Dale, but he's no dancer."

"So I am good for something," Joe said as he whirled Kathleen across the floor.

"Some things, yes." Kathleen smiled.

Josh and Scott joined Stephanie and Michelle.

"I hope they play something besides this music so we can dance," Scott said.

"I kind of like it. Look at your mom and my dad." Stephanie nudged Scott and nodded in their direction.

"There's something I've been wondering about the night of Scott's accident," Joe said as they danced.

"Oh, what about it?" Kathleen asked.

"When the hospital called, they said the family had requested their pastor. When I got there, Esther was surprised to see me."

"So?"

"So, I was wondering, who was it told them to call me?"

"That would be me," Kathleen looked away from him.

"So, I'm your pastor now?"

"The only pastor I know. Is that all right?"

"Yes, only I thought maybe I was more than your pastor. I thought, maybe, we were friends."

"Yes, we are friends," Kathleen agreed as Joe twirled her under his arm and back.

"But then I thought maybe, we were more than friends?"

"Maybe," Kathleen smiled as Joe reached down, their lips meeting.

"Maybe," Kathleen repeated. "But that doesn't mean you'll be seeing me in church any time soon."

"I wouldn't think of it," Joe said as their lips locked together in another kiss.

EPILOGUE

Having claimed Thanksgiving as her own, Esther was not about to relinquish it. Dale and Ava were fine with that. Neither wanted the task. Ava was spending her first Thanksgiving with Dale and his kids. She joined the men in the front room watching football before dinner as she cheered on her Nebraska Cornhuskers.

"It wouldn't be the same without you," Esther had told Sara, persuading her and Larry to come with the babies. Mary and Tom joined them as well. This year, Pastor Joe came with his daughters.

"You can never have too much family," Esther insisted. Peter had invited his daughters, but they were busy with their own families. His mother remained in rehab, making slow progress. Howard was joining his son's family in North Carolina for Thanksgiving before visiting his sister in Florida.

"But I'll be back to help at the Center in time for the Christmas recital," he had told them before he left, "No breakdowns allowed while I'm gone."

Stephanie and Scott were seniors, eager to get out of high school and on with their lives. The Center continued to struggle to raise necessary funds, but at least now, Kathleen was getting a paycheck.

Joe led them in grace before the meal. "Dear Lord, we are so grateful for the many blessings that have been ours this year. For new life, Angela and Gabriel, for new friends and family members. We also remember those who are unable to be with us today. We remember Joy and thank you for the time that we had with this good woman. We pray for Peter's mother, Nan, for her continued recovery and restoration to good health, and that you will bless her with many more good years." Joe paused.

"Can we eat now?" Jacob asked.

"I'm almost done, Jacob," Joe replied, and then finished with, "Bless all of us gathered around this table, bless our time together and bless this food we are about to share. Amen."

"Amen," all said in agreement.

Sara's parents left shortly after dinner. The teens escaped to the basement to watch TV and play cards. The rest finished up in the kitchen before the now traditional glass of champagne. Esther and Peter poured out the champagne and distributed the glasses to Kathleen and Joe, Dale and Ava, Sara and Larry as their group expanded to include two new members. Gabriel and Angela slept in their car seats after the noise and excitement of the afternoon.

Joe raised his glass, "Here's to remembering the past while embracing the future!"

"You sound like a Hallmark card." Kathleen shook her head as she smiled at him.

"How about to second chances and new beginnings," Peter suggested.

They clinked glasses as they said, "To new beginnings!"

DISCUSSION QUESTIONS FOR *A SLOW WALTZ*

1. The characters in *A Slow Waltz* grieve over Joy's death in their own way. Which character do you relate to the most?

2. Have you ever lost a loved one? How did you grieve that loss? How was that situation similar or different from the situation in this book?

3. Forgiveness plays an important role in healing for a number of the characters in this book. What has been your experience of forgiveness in your life? Are you in need of forgiveness?

4. "Healing is a slow process. It's a slow waltz. Sometimes you go backwards, sometimes sideways before you go forward again. It can't be rushed. But it can help if you have others by your side," Pastor Joe tells Ava. How does this healing play out in the lives of the main characters? What has been your experience of healing? Is there any area in your life that needs to be healed?

Note to the reader:

Did you enjoy reading this book? If so, please leave a review on Amazon. Your comments would be appreciated and mean so much to me in terms of helping others notice my book. You, the reader, have the power to make or break a book in this day of emarketing and social media.

Thank you so much for reading *A Slow Waltz*. While this is the final book in Joy's Trilogy, there will be more adventures for the Reese family and friends. Stay tuned for the next book in the Dancing Through Life series!

Patricia M. Robertson

Other novels by Patricia M. Robertson

Dreamweavers – Dream again, wherever you are in your life.

Buying Time – Visit the peace movement during the Cold War era of Ronald Regan, SDI (Strategic Defense Initiative) and MAD (Mutually Assured Destruction).

Land of Deep Waters - Honduras, land of deep waters, a country torn apart by civil unrest, violence and poverty: Is it possible to go back?

Magnificent Failure - Is it possible to start over? Failures in the eyes of the world and their own eyes, Diane and Jake found each other.

Dancing Through Life Series

Dancing on a High Wire – What do you do when life knocks you off balance? Join Sara, Joy and Esther aseach seeks to find a "new normal" and regain their balance on this high wire we call life.

Still Dancing - Some phone calls we love, others we hate, like the ones Pastor Joe receives from his daughter's school. Or the one Dale received at work, letting him know his wife, Joy, had fallen and was in route to the hospital by ambulance. Could her cancer be back?

An Irish Slip-Step-- Kathleen didn't know the slip jig, but she knew about slipping up. As did Chloe's, whose life was knocked off balance when her dancing career was side-lined by an unplanned pregnancy. And then there was that fiery red-head, Helen, who had crossed the Atlantic as an Irish war bride. Was it a slip-step or one of life's fortuitous missteps that brought them precisely where they were meant to be?

Robertson also is author of a companion non-fiction book to *Still Dancing, Walking With Families through the Dying Process*, as well as other non-fiction books, a weekly blog and monthly newsletter. She has a Doctor of Ministry and over thirty-five years of experience in ministry to families. For more information about her ministry go to www.patriciamrobertson.com.

An Irish Slip Step

Chapter 1

The young woman stared out the cracked window of the Brooklyn walk-up as flakes of falling snow melted on the ledge and streets below. She pushed back a strand of hair from her face and placed her hand on her expanding waist.

How did she get here? This was not the life she had envisioned when she first came to New York. Then she had been sure her dreams were about to come true. She would work hard until she was discovered and pulled from the chorus line into stardom. She had joined the ranks of so many young people, auditioning for parts, working as a waitress, waiting for the magical break-through.

So far, over the past five years, she had been in two touring companies and three Broadway productions but never made it beyond the chorus line. Now, her dancing days were over, at least until after the birth of her baby.

She didn't know why she kept the baby. The father was another acting hopeful, currently on the road and barely able to support himself. She had considered an abortion. Her friends had encouraged her to do this.

"A baby will change everything. You won't be able to support yourself. You won't be able to tour with a baby. You'll never make it," they told her.

She had thought about it, but it never seemed like the right time so she kept putting it off until it was too late. Another decision made by default, she told herself. She couldn't bring herself to do it, even though she hadn't embraced motherhood either. So here she was, five months away from giving birth. She wasn't ready.

"Couldn't you give me more time, God? More time to make it as a star? Then I could quit for a while in order to focus on motherhood," she prayed, but God didn't answer. Or if He did, she couldn't hear Him. She was running out of time.

She looked at the small Christmas tree sitting on the end table in the corner of the one bedroom apartment she shared with another acting hopeful. The one bedroom had been converted into a two bedroom by portioning off part of the living room, providing some small semblance of privacy. The tree was the only acknowledgement of the season she had allowed herself. Under its bare branches was a simple crèche, Mary, Joseph and a baby.

"How did you do it?' Chloe asked the small statuette in blue. "You weren't married when you were pregnant, but at least you had Joseph, and you had other family members. I have no one. How can I do it?" She regretted her decision not to decide about an abortion. "It seems I've been drifting through life. How can I raise a child by myself? A baby changes everything," she repeated the words of her friends.

"You can give the baby up for adoption," one of her fellow aspiring actors had suggested. "Lose your baby fat and you can be back on the circuit in a few months. There are even people willing to pay all your expenses and more for a healthy baby."

Chloe had ignored that suggestion as well. So here she was with growing debt and only her waitress tips and wages to pay the bills.

Could she go home, she wondered. She looked at her phone. Her parents were just a call away, or were they? Would they welcome their prodigal daughter? She had not left on good terms, had not kept in touch. Could she show up now, take the bus back home? Mary had made the trip to Bethlehem while pregnant with Jesus. Maybe she could do it too. All she need do is pick up the phone, call her parents and get on the bus.

Chloe stared at the phone, then dialed the number of the one person she knew she could count on.

"Grandpa?"